The Tale of
Despereaux

The Tale of Despereaux

A JUNIOR NOVELIZATION

WRITTEN BY

JAMIE MICHALAK

BASED ON THE MOTION PICTURE SCREENPLAY

AND

BASED ON THE BOOK BY

KATE DiCAMILLO

CANDLEWICK PRESS

The Rat

Come a little closer.

Get comfortable. You know what I mean: settle in, take off your coat, have a seat. You are about to hear a story. It begins like this:

Once upon a time, there was a brave little mouse who loved honor and justice and always told the truth. . . .

It was the sunniest of days. Light streamed through white, fluffy clouds and danced on the sea below, bouncing off the water in a million tiny sparkles.

It was a quiet sort of day. The kind of day when all that could be heard was the lulling rush of waves and the cries of seagulls swooping down and skimming the water's surface.

Then an enormous ship came crashing through the waves. Its tall masts reached for the sun, and its large, white sails snapped in the breeze. The wooden deck creaked as the bow sliced through the water.

On board, the ship was full of activity. Everywhere were the common sights of sailing life: winches, cannons, peg legs, and tattoos. Thick arms pulled hard on even thicker ropes. Sailors grunted and shouted.

But if you looked *very* closely, you'd see something most unexpected: Amid the action, a small rodent lay fast asleep.

Strangely, it was not lurking in some dark

nook. Instead, it was basking in the bright sunlight, curled up on deck in plain sight.

As the massive ship settled in after tacking, the creature awoke. It got up, stretched, and yawned. It raised its pointed snout toward the sun, letting the light wash over it, and took a deep breath of salty air. Then it looked around as if searching for someone.

The crew was just beginning to relax. Men grabbed a seat on barrels or huge coils of rope. Some lit their pipes. One played the pennywhistle, and its tune wafted out over the deck while the waves rocked the boat rhythmically.

The creature ran across the deck toward the sailors. It boldly approached a man who sat whittling a small figure. Even more shocking, the brazen little rodent was soon settled comfortably upon the man's shoulder.

"Tell me that thing again," it said into the sailor's ear. "Please?"

The sailor, whose name was Pietro, smiled

warmly at the all-too-familiar request. "Oh, come on, Roscuro."

Ah! you might be thinking, *Roscuro must be the "brave little mouse."*

No. That's not him.

That's a rat.

And anyone who knows anything knows there's a big difference between a mouse and a rat.

First of all, rats hate the light. They spend their lives in darkness. They're also terrified of people, which is why they slink and cower all the time. And as far as "telling the truth" is concerned, well, that's impossible, because as everyone knows, a rat can't talk. And *yet* . . .

"Just once, I promise," Roscuro said, leaning forward. "Tell me one more time, and I won't ask you ever again. I swear."

Pietro sighed. "Fine. We are headed to Dor, one of the most magical places in the whole world."

"No, that is not what you said before," said

Roscuro, shaking his head. "You know, 'Every place has something special . . .'"

"That *is* what I said."

"No, it is *not*," Roscuro insisted. "Remember what you said? It was so great." Roscuro stood up straight as if making a pronouncement: "'Every place we go has something special about it, and in Dor, it's the soup.'"

"See? You know it," said Pietro.

"Yeah, but not like you do. Come on! 'Not just any soup . . .'" Roscuro continued dramatically, "'*Amazing* soup. *Incredible* soup. In fact, after you taste one spoonful, you will never want to have any other soup again for the rest of your life!'"

"So what do you need *me* for?" Pietro asked, amused.

Roscuro sighed in frustration. He was just about to protest Pietro's infuriating stubbornness when a joyful voice called out, "LAND, HO!"

The boat creaked and turned. The sailors

jumped to attention and hurried about the deck.

At once, Roscuro jumped off Pietro's shoulder and raced up the nearest rope. He leaped from spar to spar, scurried across the sails, and nimbly crossed one of the lines, working his way up the mast, all the way to the crow's nest.

In an instant, Roscuro had reached the top, where one of the ship's flags flew. He put a small paw to his forehead and scanned the horizon. His eyes lit up.

"I can see it!" Roscuro called down.

Pietro, the only one who could hear Roscuro's voice, glanced up at his tiny friend.

The seafaring rat had seen many places in his life, but the place Roscuro saw at this moment thrilled him like no other. His heart leaped at the sight of it. And whose wouldn't?

The Kingdom of Dor was like a little jewel glistening against the sea. The castle—and everything around it—seemed to radiate light.

Shimmering towers rose majestically into the sky. Their golden spires glowed warmly like a king's crown. At the base of white cliffs, a small harbor twinkled in the sunlight, and ships bobbed happily at anchor. Dor looked as if it had been sprinkled liberally with a giant shaker of stardust.

To a rat who loved light, Dor was a magical place indeed.

But there was something else. Something amazing.

Roscuro sniffed, and sniffed again.

Something incredible.

"Ooh, I can *smell* it! I can smell it!" Roscuro cried, inhaling more deeply.

Something that would change the rat's life forever.

CHAPTER TWO

Royal Soup Day

What the rat smelled was soup, of course.

Yes, soup.

Now, this was not your everyday soup smell. The aroma of this soup was so magical, so heavenly, so out-of-this-world intoxicating that, the moment the ship docked, the smell lifted Roscuro up by his whiskered nose and led him off the gangplank, straight into the Kingdom of Dor.

The street was a line of endless soup shops. The Iron Kettle, Benjamin's Broth House, the

Steaming Stewpot, the Magic Ladle. . . . Roscuro couldn't decide where to begin.

What's more, Dorian men, women, and children streamed down the street carrying huge bowls and spoons.

"Oh, I can't wait to taste this soup!" Roscuro told Pietro.

He was perched upon Pietro's shoulder and peering eagerly into the shop windows. But to the rat's confusion, the soup shops were all closing early. *Why* today, *of all days?* Roscuro wondered, devastated.

"Just stay close," warned Pietro. "We leave at six."

"You know, we ought to think about staying here a little longer," Roscuro suggested.

"Don't even think about it. Remember Shanghai?" Pietro reminded him.

"Yeah, but this place is different. I mean, this is special. This place is . . ." the rat struggled for the right word. "It's . . . it's, you know . . . it's . . ."

Strange?

Well, maybe a little. But it certainly smelled good to Roscuro.

On any given day, just a whiff from one of the soup shops was almost like having a full meal. But on one very special day every year, the Kingdom of Dor was transformed.

As if by fate, Roscuro and Pietro happened to visit Dor on that very day. Although they didn't know it. Not yet. All they knew at that moment was that they wanted soup.

So when another shop owner flipped an OPEN sign to CLOSED and hurried in the same direction as the others, Pietro and Roscuro followed close behind.

In Dor, Christmas was nothing compared to Royal Soup Day.

In the town square, Pietro and Roscuro joined the hundreds of villagers who gathered in anxious anticipation of their favorite holiday. Roscuro was delighted by what he saw.

Towers of bowls and spoons teetered upon tables. A soup-kettle band performed classic soup songs. Old men played the spoons, and two groups of red-faced folks shouted at each other.

"Bisque!" yelled one side.

"Chowder!" yelled the other.

"BISQUE!"

"CHOWDER!"

On Royal Soup Day, every Dorian, young and old, flocked toward the castle, because they knew that at this very moment, deep within the royal kitchens, a masterpiece was being created. . . .

The royal kitchen staff could hear the crowd outside their window growing louder and more restless. But there was no time to peek at the spectacle. Not while they were so behind on this year's soup. And definitely not with Chef André breathing down their necks.

The kitchen was abuzz with activity. Every space was crammed with moving conveyor belts, steaming cauldrons, and machines of every kind. Machines that sliced, diced, and chopped. Machines that stirred, whipped, and whirled. Olive pitters, seed pluckers, eggplant peelers, turnip sorters, and even a special flame-throwing machine used solely for charring the skins of bell peppers.

In the center of this madness stood Chef André, overseeing each and every step.

"More onions!" he ordered, shaking his head in dissatisfaction. "How many times do I have to say it?"

His nervous crew scurried.

"More onions, more onions, more ONIONS!" they repeated.

Everyone knew Chef André was a genius, but they were reminded of it on the first

Sunday of every spring. At exactly twelve noon, he would unveil that year's special creation.

Until then, the Dorian mob jammed the town square, waiting for the king to make his announcement. And as the aroma began to build, they speculated as to the contents of this year's masterpiece.

The suspense was killing them. But in many ways, it was also their favorite part.

"C'mon, me lovelies, place your bets!" a bookie called to the crowd. "Bisque, three to one. Broth, five to one. Seafood chowder a long shot at twenty-five to one."

This year seemed more tense than ever, on account of the scrumptious scent wafting out of the castle. When Roscuro got his first whiff of the aroma, he could think of nothing else.

Where, oh *where*, was the soup? he kept wondering.

And so was everyone else, when at last they saw movement on the royal balcony.

The king stepped out to a thunderous

cheer. Next came the queen, and then the princess.

"Wow," whispered Roscuro, smitten.

Princess Pea sparkled with light, from her shiny, golden hair to her sequined dress that twinkled in the sun.

The king raised his hands to quiet the crowd.

"Welcome, friends—friends of soup," he greeted them. "Now, the moment you've all been waiting for. Princess Pea, the envelope, please."

As the king took the envelope from his daughter, you could practically hear hundreds of stomachs growling. Everyone smacked their lips with anticipation.

"It is my pleasure," said the king, "to announce this year's royal creation from the kitchen of Chef André. . . ."

CHAPTER THREE

The Chef's Secret

In the royal kitchen, all was still. The staff held their breath and crossed their fingers behind their backs. André was about to taste this year's royal soup.

The chef brought the spoon to his lips. He rolled the broth around in his mouth. And then, with difficulty, he swallowed.

"NO, NO, NO!" André exploded. "Something is wrong. I need more time!"

"But we're late already," said a panicked sous-chef.

As if on cue, a loud ovation erupted outside. The king was about to open the envelope.

"Zis is not RIGHT! Everyone out! OUT!" André ordered, chasing his trembling staff from the kitchen.

When he was certain that they were gone, André stormed into a back room of the royal kitchen—his own secret laboratory. Whatever went on within those walls was a mystery to all but him.

Slamming the door behind him, André crossed over to his large work table, which was hidden under piles of hacked-up vegetables, mixing bowls, and an assortment of kitchen gadgets only André could understand.

He glanced behind him at a high shelf in the corner. He sniffed, and then paused as if considering something.

Now, a big part of being a genius is making everyone believe that you are. And sometimes that takes a little help.

André dragged a small footstool over to the bookshelf and climbed on top of it. He reached up to the highest ledge, and from its farthest corner, pulled down a decrepit leather tome.

The book seemed ordinary enough. But once André opened it, a peculiar thing began to happen.

A strange spirit rose into the air, a rainbow of herbs, vegetables, pots, and pans swirling above the tabletop. The colorful pieces fit together to form a hovering figure made of food and kitchen utensils.

There are all kinds of genies. Some are in lamps; some are in bottles. But what else would live inside a cookbook but a soup genie?

The genie, whose name was Boldo, grinned at the angry chef below him.

"You changed some-sing," André accused him.

"You're crazy. I did not touch it," said Boldo.

"I can smell it." André inspected the genie,

from lettuce hair to tomato cheeks to string-bean fingers. "Hmm . . . what's zis?"

"What?" Boldo asked innocently.

"ZIS!" André said, plucking a garlic clove from Boldo's chest.

"Ouch!" cried Boldo. "Garlic."

"Garlic," André repeated.

Boldo shrugged. "Yeah, there's a little garlic. It was already there."

"No," said André.

"Yes," said Boldo.

"NO!"

"YES!"

"Not zis much," said André. He pulled a string of garlic from Boldo's waist. "You ruined my soup."

"I saved your soup. Those people wait a whole year, and you want to give them this dishwater?" said Boldo.

"Dishwater?"

"Dish. Water."

"DISHWATER?" André roared. He yanked a large onion from Boldo's face.

"Ow, cut it out!" Boldo whined.

Meanwhile, in the town square, the king opened the envelope.

"And this year's soup," he read, oblivious to the chaos in the kitchen, "is a spring tureen of fresh herbs, roasted vegetables, and wild mushrooms."

A huge cheer erupted from the crowd. At last, the soup was ready!

But Roscuro could wait no longer. Hypnotized by the soup's aroma, he jumped off Pietro's shoulder and scurried up the castle walls.

At the door to André's private room, the sous-chefs listened as the argument raged on.

"I don't have to stand here and listen to a big talking garbage can!" André snarled.

"Ha! And I don't have to listen to a coward!" yelled Boldo.

"Coward?"

"Yes, a coward."

"Call me a COWARD?"

"Yes."

André ripped another clove of garlic from Boldo.

Enraged, the soup genie pulled a tomato off his own ear and threw it at the chef, hitting André square in the apron. *SPLAT!*

André picked up a rolling pin and sent it flying at Boldo.

Boldo grabbed an onion from his chest.

Soon bowls, spoons, and pans flew across the room in every direction. Bottles smashed against the walls. The floor was quickly covered in crushed produce, broken glass, and gadgets. Ripped cookbooks lay everywhere.

Amid the wreckage, André fumed. He

picked up the last unbroken object—a bottle of wine—and hurled it with all his strength at Boldo.

The bottle shot like a bullet straight for the genie's head.

Boldo ducked. The bottle sailed right past him and landed—*splash!*—in the cauldron of finished soup. The soup that every Dorian, including the royal family, was demanding at that very minute.

André and Boldo looked at each other in horror.

"Uh-oh," said Boldo.

The two approached the pot slowly.

"Oh no, no, no, no, no, no, no," André moaned.

This was a problem. A royal disaster. The soup was surely ruined. What was Royal Soup Day without soup?

Hesitantly, André and Boldo neared the cauldron.

They sniffed.

They paused.

They sniffed again.

Not bad, André thought. He put a tentative finger into the soup and tasted it. His eyes widened.

Boldo dipped a string-bean finger and tried it as well. *Hmm, pretty good*, he thought.

Was it possible? André and Boldo exchanged a look. They tasted the soup again. This time, they each heartily plunged a whole spoon into the broth and savored the new taste.

Of course, they thought. *WINE!*

"*Bellissima*," said Boldo, embracing André.

"It's *fantastique!*" said André. And in a rare display of affection, André kissed Boldo on each cheek, squashing two tomatoes.

But while Chef André and Boldo rejoiced high up in the castle, a very different scene was unfolding down below. Pietro frantically searched the village streets for his little friend.

"Roscuro? Roscuro?" Pietro called, jostling with pedestrians. "Roscuro? Roscuro? Where are you? ROSCURO?"

It was no use.

Roscuro was gone.

CHAPTER FOUR

Roscuro Meets the Queen

So how do you find a rat half-mad with desire for soup?

You follow your nose.

While Pietro was combing every nook and cranny of the village, Roscuro was clinging to the castle ballroom's chandelier.

Why? you ask. Because below him, the royal soup was about be served for the first time.

Roscuro waited, salivating.

Far beneath him, a long, candlelit table was set for an opulent banquet. The king sat proudly, with the queen and princess at either side, at the end of the crowded table.

They, too, were waiting. All eyed the royal kitchen's door, eager to see their genius chef come through with his latest creation.

When the door finally opened, the guests rose to their feet and clapped furiously. André entered carrying a large porcelain soup tureen, which he ceremoniously placed in front of the queen.

Ever so slowly, André lifted the china lid.

"Ooooooh!" exclaimed the crowd.

Princess Pea and her mother leaned forward in anticipation.

So did Roscuro. He leaned forward on the chandelier, trying to take in as much of the soup's mouth-watering scent as he could. When the fragrant steam finally reached his nose, he closed his eyes and crinkled his little rat nostrils in bliss.

"Voilà!" said André.

"This smells amazing," said the queen, beaming.

"Wait until Your Highness tastes it."

The queen dipped her spoon into the broth.

Roscuro sniffed. His mouth watered. He inched closer and closer still, until he was holding on to the chandelier by a single little paw.

The spoon hovered near the queen's mouth. She parted her lips and took her first delicious taste.

"Mmmmm!" she said, sighing.

Roscuro could only imagine the sensation. His eyes closed again, and a dreamy smile lit up his face as he imagined the unique blend of tastes. He reeled back in reverie. Then, just as quickly, Roscuro slipped and lost his grip on the chandelier.

Roscuro's eyes opened wide. The air rushed

past his ears, flattening his whiskers to his cheeks. He was falling, falling to the table below!

At the very moment the queen was savoring her first taste, the soup-crazed rat was tumbling head over feet, feet over head until . . .

"André," the queen said, "this is absolutely de—"

SPLAT!

Roscuro landed with a walloping belly flop in the queen's soup.

"It moved!" the queen exclaimed.

"It moved?" André asked.

"My soup MOVED!" the queen said.

André eyed the soup. "No, it didn't. It did not move."

But the chef could not argue when the rat surfaced from the broth wearing a ring of onion around his head. Roscuro wiped broth from his eyes and looked straight at the queen.

"Oh, Your Highness," the rat greeted her.

"AHHHHH!" squealed the queen.

"Darling?" said her husband.

"A RAT!" she screeched. "There is a RAT in my soup!"

Why does she say "rat" as if it's a bad word? Roscuro wondered.

"Madam," said Roscuro politely, "I know that this is unfortunate, and I know that while on first glance I might appear to be —"

"AHHHHH!" the queen screamed. "A RAT! THERE IS A RAT IN MY SOUP!"

"Please. . . . Shh," whispered Roscuro.

The queen looked down at him in horror. "AND I ATE IT!" she cried.

"Uh-oh," said Roscuro.

The queen began to gag. She clutched at her throat as the color drained from her face. She swooned. Roscuro barely managed to leap out of the way before Her Highness lurched — first backward, then forward — and nose-dived into her bowl of soup.

The shocked party did not know where to look first—at Their Royal Highness facedown in her vegetable soup, *dead*, or at the drenched rat who had just sprung onto the linen tablecloth.

"She's right!" yelled the king, pointing at the exposed Roscuro. "It's a rat!"

"Ahh, it's a rat!" squealed Princess Pea, and then seeing her mother, she let out a piercing scream.

"Sweetie, scrumptious?" the king said to his fallen wife. He turned toward his guards. "GET ME THAT RAT!"

Roscuro sprinted down the center of the banquet table. He hopped over place settings. He darted around a candlestick, leaped over a finger bowl, and vaulted off a salad fork as if it were a diving board.

"Now, I really believe you are jumping to conclusions," Roscuro tried to explain breathlessly, hurtling over the centerpiece, "and I am sure other rats you have met might have caused you to create a stereotype. . . . I'm just, I'm not really from around here. Oh!"

A large steak knife missed his tail by an inch. "Ooohh, that is very aggressive," he cried.

At the end of the table, Roscuro slid down the tablecloth as if it were the rigging of his ship. He scurried across the floor.

"The kitchen!" André shouted to the guards. "He's going into the KITCHEN!"

Roscuro fled through the kitchen door as a dozen armored men scrambled after him.

CHAPTER FIVE

The Hunt for a Rat

"Over there!" yelled a guard.

Roscuro raced across the floor with the guards' large metal boots stomping close behind him. Where to hide?

He darted into a pile of pots and pans. Their curved metal edges reflected Roscuro's body over and over. Roscuro felt as if he were in an endless hall of mirrors. In the reflections, Roscuro looked huge and grotesque. He felt dizzy, fumbling his way through the many monstrous images, when —

"STOP THAT RAT!" André screamed, racing toward him.

A sword whizzed by Roscuro's head. Its blade missed him by a whisker. Pots and pans tumbled to the floor.

SWISH! BANG! CRASH!

Roscuro bounded off the edge of the shelf and into a metal mixing bowl. He slid down its sloped interior and up the other side and hurtled through the air again.

Oof! Roscuro landed on a table near a pile of vegetables. He stopped next to a carrot to catch his breath.

WHAP!

A massive blade came down next to him, chopping the carrot cleanly in half. Roscuro clutched his heart in terror and checked to see if he was still in one piece. *That could have been ME!* he thought. *Why are they trying to kill me? What have I done?*

But there was no time for thinking. A blade landed again with a loud *CHOP* that sent Roscuro scurrying down the center of the table.

He leaped from onion to onion. Over a hill of potatoes. Through a forest of celery.

SMACK! SWISH! WHACK!

The blade sliced down again.

Roscuro spotted some sausage links hanging from a rack. He grabbed for one and swung from salami to salami with the clanking metal of the guards ringing in his ears.

"He's going near THE SOUP!" yelled André. "There's a rat loose in my KITCHEN!"

Roscuro was almost out of sausages. He pounced onto a whisk dangling from a hook. Roscuro parted the wires and slipped inside. Finally safe!

He slumped against the whisk's wires and tried to catch his breath. But not a moment later, a large eye appeared beside him. A guard was peering through the wires like a giant looking in a window.

"Ahhh!" Roscuro screamed. "If I can just, just tell—"

The guard grabbed the whisk and wielded

it like a mace. Roscuro swung upside down, as if on some twisted carnival ride, and flew from the whisk. He sailed through the air and landed on the guard's metal boot.

The guard impulsively swung at Roscuro with his mace, bashing his own foot.

"Owwwww!" he howled, leaping up and down with pain.

Roscuro raced across the floor. With nowhere left to go, he climbed up a long metal vegetable chute. He scaled it to the kitchen's highest point, where a small window overlooked the port.

Outside, something in the distance caught Roscuro's attention. Even under the circumstances, he could not help but stop and stare.

Far beyond Roscuro's reach was his ship. It had weighed anchor and was beginning to sail away . . . with Pietro on board!

He pressed his paws to the glass. *Noooooo!* the rat wanted to cry. *Stop! Please don't go! Pietro!*

Roscuro's heart sank. Helpless, he gazed out at his old friend, desperately wishing for him to come back.

So lost was the rat in his own thoughts, he had nearly forgotten he was in terrible danger, when suddenly — *SPLAT!* — he was reminded by a large tomato that whooshed past his head and smashed against the windowpane. The crushed tomato dripped down the glass, obscuring the view of Pietro and the ship.

Roscuro jumped back. He lost his balance and slid down the chute toward the huge cauldron of soup.

"No, no, no!" yelled André. "Not there!"

Without a second to spare, André lifted the chute, changing the rat's path. Roscuro catapulted across the kitchen.

He landed hard on the stone floor and looked up to see four of the king's guards. To Roscuro, they were giants with feet as big as houses. They were stepping closer and closer, their sharp swords jabbing and jabbing.

Roscuro ducked right, then left, then right again as the swords sliced down within a breath of his body.

The blows rained down one after another. The guards backed Roscuro onto a grate near the wall, and then there was nowhere to go but down.

SWISH! SMACK!

Roscuro slipped between the grate's bars. He grabbed blindly for one of them and clutched it with a paw. The rat hung on for his life, until . . .

SMACK!

Roscuro plummeted down, down, down. . . .

CHAPTER SIX

Darkness

Roscuro blinked. Then blinked again as his eyes tried to adjust to the awful darkness. But it didn't help. The rat had landed in a place of suffocating, stifling blackness. And for a rat who loved daylight, this was a terrible place indeed.

Roscuro looked up toward the grate, now stories above him, where one last trickle of light struggled to reach him. He could see little: a faint outline of damp, rancid walls; a steep staircase that lead down into yet more darkness; and his reflection in a puddle.

He stared down at his face, the same one that had caused the queen so much terror. Was he that ugly? he wondered. That repulsive? He thrust his paw into the water, destroying his reflection.

Roscuro slumped against the wall and sat for a while, trying to muster the courage to move. But for what? he asked himself. He was a rat. A rat without a home, or a friend. He was alone. Completely alone. . . . And then the rat did something most unratlike.

The rat began to cry.

Roscuro cried. And cried. And cried.

And he didn't stop crying until he felt something. Or rather, *someone.* Roscuro felt an icy prickling at the back of his neck. The kind of feeling you get when you're being watched.

Roscuro froze as the shadow of a towering, robed figure emerged from the darkness. Two red eyes slowly materialized.

And then, behind that creature, more eyes. Roscuro squeaked and hid behind his paws.

"You don't need to be afraid," the creature said, slinking from the shadows and into the gray light. It had the face of a rodent, but it was much, much taller with long, gangly arms and fingerlike claws.

"I know it's dark," the creature soothed, "but you'll get used to it."

"Who—who are you?" Roscuro asked, blinking.

The grotesque face inched closer. It was horrid—gnarled and fanged with sunken eyes.

"Just a rat, like you," he said. His name was Botticelli, and he was the most frightening rat Roscuro had ever seen.

"Come with me," Botticelli said, with a creepy smile.

Botticelli draped one long arm around the smaller rat's shoulder. Roscuro rose slowly and let the stranger lead him deeper into the dungeon.

CHAPTER SEVEN

Waiting for a Hero

The Queen of Dor was laid to rest in the royal chapel.

Princess Pea, luminescent even in grief, bid her mother a final farewell. In her hand she held a familiar object, which she tenderly placed at her mother's grave: the queen's soup bowl.

Then the king stepped forward, and with tears filling his eyes, placed a flower in the empty bowl.

Grief is the strongest thing that a person can feel. You don't feel it often, but when you do . . .

And death can feel so unfair, as if someone has taken something from you, as if it's been stolen. When something hurts this much, there must be a reason. There must be someone to blame.

A hurt king, looking to blame someone, can be a dangerous person. His wife's body had no sooner been laid to rest than the king sat down in his chambers to write—and to punish.

The village crier read the king's proclamation in the town square:

From this moment on, soup—the making of soup, the selling of soup, or the eating of soup—is hereby outlawed in the Kingdom of Dor. Rats are to be considered illegal as well and are hereby deemed unlawful creatures in the Kingdom of Dor. From this moment on, anyone harboring, sheltering, or possessing a rat in any way shall face the full wrath of the law.

As decreed, the royal guards collected every soup kettle, spoon, and dish. They even confiscated the dogs' bowls.

In the royal kitchen, André's big soup pot was covered up.

In shops and homes, rats were chased and hunted.

And in his chambers, the king played the same sad, wailing notes on his guitar over and over.

So think about this. What happens when something that is just a natural part of the world is suddenly made illegal? You may as well make flies illegal, or sweat, or Monday mornings. But that's what the king did — out of a terrible sadness.

Dor's once vibrant village was now silent, its town square empty. Soup kettles piled up in the gutters along the entire length of the street.

Sunlight left, and the world went gray. Colors faded into one another, and dark clouds filled the sky. And for a long time it wouldn't rain. The clouds just stayed. And stayed. And stayed.

In her bedroom, Princess Pea stared out across the bleak landscape.

Louise, her maid, was fitting the princess for a dress, and the jeweled gown threw sequined light all around the room. But Pea did not notice.

"I wish it would rain," said Pea. She looked at the trees, now dead and lifeless under the gloomy sky. Summer, fall, winter, spring—gray reigned all year.

"You an' the whole world," Louise replied, accidentally sticking Pea with a needle.

"Ow!" said Pea, wincing.

"Sorry, milady," Louise apologized.

"Well, at least I can still feel that." Pea turned back to her window. "Louise? Do you think there's a bit of light somewhere in the world?"

"Dunno, ma'am," said Louise.

"I think there is. You just need to know where to find it," said Pea.

But that was the dilemma. Where do you find light in a land where the thing its people love most has been banned?

Because in the royal kitchen, soup no longer bubbled in cauldrons. Magical aromas did not fill the air. Every ingredient was stored away and every pot neatly stacked. What was once a happy mess was now tidy and sterile.

The bustling kitchen staff had dwindled to one member. André, depressed and alone, sat at his table, idly spinning a Dorian shilling.

On the third spin, he accidentally flicked the small shilling onto the floor. But the chef made no movement to get it. He just watched the coin roll to the corner of the room and disappear into a mousehole.

Do you remember when we told you that *once upon a time, there was a brave little mouse*? Well, if you know anything about fairy tales, you know that a hero doesn't appear until the world really needs one.

CHAPTER EIGHT

The Mouse

Small, warm lights began to appear in the windows of homes, from the distant hillside cottages nestled on the storeroom's shelves to the thickly settled houses in town.

In the shadow of a tall bell tower, the lamplighter was making his rounds. He illuminated a long row of matchsticks, the mouse version of gas lamps, along the edge of the town square.

Evening was usually a quiet time in town, a time of walking slowly and talking softly. But this evening, Lester Tilling was doing neither.

"Excuse me. . . . Oh. . . . Excuse me. . . . Excuse me. . . . Sorry," he apologized, as he scurried past couples strolling arm in arm.

(Lester Tilling happened to be very good at both apologizing and scurrying. This was fortunate because he was in a desperate hurry and crashing into everyone in his path.)

He anxiously weaved through the evening strollers and turned left at the end of the square.

"Sorry. . . ." Lester mumbled, scurrying on.

"Tilling?" came a stern voice.

Lester skittered to a halt. He looked up to find that he was in front of the Mouse Council Courthouse. And before him stood none other than the mayor.

"Oh, Mr. Mayor. Hello," Lester said breathlessly.

The mayor looked down his whiskered nose at the quivering mess that was Lester Tilling. "Where are you going?"

"Oh . . . well . . . my baby is having a . . .

I mean, my wife is going to be a . . ."

"Oh, right," said the mayor. "Congratulations."

"Thank you. Thank you, sir. I am sorry. . . .
I really . . ." Lester sputtered, but the mayor
was already walking away. "Good-bye," Lester
said, nodding nervously.

As soon as the mayor passed from sight,
Lester sighed in relief and took off again at full
scurry. He raced all the way to a long, curved
road of row houses, each similarly decorated,
each almost exactly alike. And into one of
those homes, Lester disappeared.

Lester Tilling burst through his front door to
find three mice huddled together. His wife,
Antoinette; their son Furlough; and the doctor gathered around a soup ladle that had
been made into a cradle.

Lester joined them to see his baby mouse
for the very first time.

Antoinette studied the new mouse in the cradle. He was small. Ridiculously tiny. Smaller than Furlough had been, by far. Smaller than any mouse she'd *ever* seen.

Swaddled in a handkerchief, the new mouse would go unnoticed were it not for two exceptionally large ears standing out above the fabric.

"His eyes are *open!*" Antoinette cried to the doctor.

A rare ray of light had inexplicably found its way into the storeroom and shone directly upon the tiny mouse. More astonishing, the mouse was looking up at the light, and he was smiling.

"Don't worry about it, Antoinette. Sometimes they are," said the doctor.

"But he isn't *cowering*. He's looking right at us."

"Oh, don't worry. He'll learn to cower. They all do in time."

"But he *isn't*."

The rest of the family stared at its peculiar addition. But the mouse wasn't looking back at them. His eyes traveled all around the room, drinking in its rich detail. He seemed particularly fascinated by the walls. They were papered with an illuminated manuscript, and the mouse appeared to study its intricate gold letters.

"Mom, he's so puny," said Furlough. "And look at those ears!"

At the sound of his brother's voice, the baby mouse's enormous ears suddenly moved. They twitched. They flexed and focused on the voice in the same way a person might when noticing something for the first time. They seemed almost . . . curious.

And from the very beginning, Despereaux Tilling heard more, saw more, and experienced more than any of the other mice.

CHAPTER NINE

The First Trap

Time passed, but even when Despereaux was old enough to attend school, he had not grown much larger than when we last saw him in his cradle.

Still, Despereaux's puny size did not stop him from gathering his friends for his latest plan. They stood in a huddle just outside the mousehole.

"Despereaux, don't do it!" urged a young mouse.

The others agreed. Nobody wanted Despereaux to go through with his plan. It was dangerous and *definitely* against the rules. If the Mouse Council—and especially the mayor—found out, who knew what they would do?

Despereaux wasn't listening to his friends. His eyes remained fixed on something several feet away.

To an observer with any common sense, the mouse's mission was impossible. On one side was a wisp of a mouse. On the other, a large, loaded mousetrap. The tiny mouse would surely die—or give up.

But Despereaux charged straight at the contraption.

"Despereaux!" his friends cheered between cowers.

With a giant leap, Despereaux flung himself into the trap's jaws. He knocked the cheese clean off the trigger just as the trap's huge, lethal bar sliced through the air like a guillotine.

WHAP!

The other mice covered their eyes. They could hardly bear to see what had happened to their small friend.

Hesitantly, they peeked out from behind their trembling paws.

The bar had just missed Despereaux's neck.

He had dived for safety, landed on his head, and was righting himself when — *plunk* — down came the cheese, smack between his ears!

"All right!" whooped his friends, descending on the tasty prize.

Despereaux, however, did not look at the cheese. He was looking at the sprung mouse-trap and smiling.

Yes, Despereaux was pleased with his game, and his friends were delighted with their prize, but in beating the trap, Despereaux had done something serious. He had broken a rule. No one broke rules in the mouse world. Not on purpose, at least. The rules were everything. Rules were what kept the mice safe and what kept them so wonderfully afraid . . . of the mayor and the Mouse Council and just about everything else.

Without rules, mice might be like . . . rats.

But Despereaux wasn't scared. He was already wondering where he could find another mousetrap.

You see, Despereaux Tilling had no idea he was small. He wasn't just small in human terms. He was small even for a mouse. But to tell you the truth, he didn't even notice.

In his own mind, Despereaux was a giant.

CHAPTER TEN

What the Mouse Found

Most young mice cause their parents to worry every now and then. But most young mice do not play with mousetraps for fun. Needless to say, Mr. and Mrs. Tilling were exceptionally concerned. They decided it was time for a talk with Despereaux's teacher.

Despereaux's school stood on top of an old chess table. It was a formal-looking school-house — built from a series of leather-bound books and topped with a graduation cap — and the Tillings cowered respectfully as they entered. They found Despereaux's classroom and took a seat inside.

"We're worried about him," said Lester, sitting uncomfortably before the teacher. "He doesn't scurry. He doesn't cower. At first we thought he would grow out of it, but—"

"Well, he scurries sometimes," Antoinette interrupted.

"But not when he's scared. He just does it for fun. And he never cowers. We've showed him how, but . . ."

Despereaux's teacher smiled. "Well, some kids are slower than others. He'll cower in time. We'll work on it."

"Yes, but . . ." Lester began.

"It'll be fine. I promise," the teacher assured him.

Despereaux's teacher kept her word and began reinforcing cowering skills the very next day at school.

"All right, settle down," she ordered the rowdy mice before her. In her paws she held a large deck of flash cards. "Ready, class?"

She raised the first card for Despereaux and his classmates to see. On it was a picture of Swiss cheese.

The mice leaned forward in interest.

Then came cheddar. Again, the mice leaned forward, licking their lips.

"Good," said the teacher.

And another one. Some Brie.

"Good. Excellent."

And finally . . . *a carving knife!*

"AAAAAAAAH!" the class squealed. The mice screamed and hid under desks, covering their faces with their paws.

But Despereaux did not do any of these things. Despereaux Tilling stared straight ahead.

"Despereaux!" the teacher chided.

"Yes?"

"You didn't cower."

"Looks like a sword," he said.

"It's a *carving knife*," she said, shocked.

"It's beautiful," Despereaux said, sighing.

"It's DANGEROUS."

Despereaux smiled, savoring the word.

"Do you . . . do you have any more?" he asked.

To Despereaux, danger was delicious. So it was only a matter of time before the danger-hungry mouse found the dark edge of town and what lay in it.

This part of the mouse world was a grave-yard for everything the mice couldn't use. It was a filthy place where unwanted objects de-cayed in huge, forgotten piles, where — once in a great while — an unwanted mouse went to disappear. *Forever.*

Despereaux had spotted an iron grate there, and for some reason, it was causing an unprecedented amount of cowering among his friends. Curious, Despereaux slid down the slope that lead to the grate.

"Despereaux, what are you doing?" asked his friend. "We're not even supposed to be here. That's the DUNGEON. There are RATS down there."

"And they'll eat you!" said a second mouse.

"And pull your arms off!" added a third.

The tiny mouse neared the grate, and as he did, his ears twitched and turned toward it. Despereaux heard a distant noise coming from deep below. It was some kind of strange and horrible singing, a low chanting. Despereaux peered into the abyss. "How far down is it?"

"I don't know," said the first mouse. "No one has ever come back."

"How come?" Despereaux asked.

"'Cause—'cause . . ." the mouse said, trembling.

"'Cause that's where you go when you get—when you get b-b-b-b-b—" said the second mouse.

"Banished?" asked Despereaux, looking back toward his friends. "What do you get banished for?"

The shuddering mice gasped and talked over one another. "Oh, you know—"

"Rules and—"

"Yeah, breaking the—"

"Can't even talk about it—"

"'Cause that's one of the rules."

Surely you will not be surprised to learn that Despereaux was not paying any attention to his friends' warnings.

"Despereaux!" his friends pleaded.

"I just want to have a quick look," Despereaux said. He stopped to listen again for the chanting. Trying to make out the words as to what unspeakable horrors lay below, Despereaux walked closer to the grate. He went right up to its edge, close enough to detect a smell rising from it—a wretched, rotting, nightmarish stench.

"We gotta get out of here!" one of his friends whispered.

Despereaux crawled out onto a long plank that jutted over the grate.

The other mice shook to the tips of their ears. "Oh, my gosh . . . oh, no . . . oh, sheesh . . . uh-oh . . ." they chattered.

"Despereaux! You can't FEED 'em!" one whispered loudly.

But Despereaux was already leaning over the plank and holding out a crumb. Could the rats smell it? he wondered. Could they smell *him?*

"He-ll-o-o-o. . . ." he called. He stared into the nothingness and heard his own voice eerily return to him, *"He-ll-o-o-o. . . ."*

The other mice covered their eyes.

"Here ya go. Whoever you are," Despereaux said.

The mouse let go of the crumb and watched as the darkness swallowed it whole.

CHAPTER ELEVEN

A Rat is a Rat

The wretched, rotting, nightmarish stink that Despereaux smelled could only have come from one thing: a rat.

Far, far below the grate, two red eyes pierced the darkness. The rat happened to be fishing by the edge of an open sewer when a crumb plunked rudely upon his head.

Now if *one* rat smelled that bad, can you imagine what hundreds of them smelled like? The stench above the grate was almost pleasant compared to the vile rankness that permeated the sewer below.

You'd discover the stench only grew worse if you were to follow the filthy river snaking beneath the castle. And if you were to fumble blindly through the sewer's dank tunnel, you'd not only smell evil but *hear* it—a faint echo of drumming and chanting.

But you would never do this.

No one would. Because if you followed the tunnel to the end, you'd find yourself in a huge underground chasm, where no ray of light ever entered. You'd be in the belly of the rat world. And no one—*no one*—had ever escaped this place alive.

In fact, the rats made their very homes from the bones and skulls of their victims, the dungeon's prisoners. Like the mice, they also created a world from cast-off objects. But instead of shiny spoons and polished boxes, the rats chose the most disgusting garbage: fish skeletons, moldy food, a chicken's foot.

Within the rats' underground village, the river emptied into a large lake of raw sewage.

Boats made of lobster shells drifted aimlessly in the black waters. Across the lake, the stark outline of a coliseum dominated the horizon.

Rats entertained themselves in the littered streets. Some placed bets on a scorpion fight. They cheered loudly for their favorites as the creatures jabbed at each other viciously. Another rat sat nearby and played a flute to a bowl of worms like a snake charmer.

The streets were loud and boisterous, and the activity was only interrupted when a dinner bell suddenly rang throughout the town.

It was Feast Day, the best day of the week. The day the castle's trash was thrown down the garbage chute and into the center of the rat town square.

The rats dropped what they were doing. They ran from all over the village and streamed over a bridge made from a human backbone. Everyone headed for the mountain of garbage that had just arrived.

A tremendous fire, the village's only light, blazed in the open square. The sound in the square was deafening. A massive tangle of rats were working themselves into a frenzy.

From a raised dais made of a knight's rusted armor, Botticelli watched the rats dance and sing:

"Stinky, dark and foul and rotting,
oozing sores and blood that's clotting
Mmm! Delicious! Hits the spot!
IT'S GREAT TO BE A RAT!"

Their bodies cast dark, menacing shadows along the walls as they swarmed over a moldy garbage pile. Hundreds of rats danced around it in a circle, holding matches over their heads like giant torches.

The mob reveled, feverish, reeling wild in the torchlight, chanting ever louder as they celebrated the life of a rat:

"When we see a chained-up victim,
Our hearts bleed—and then we lick him.
Chew his ears and nose—they picked him.
WE'RE JUST BEING RATS!

Give us flesh and filth and bile.
What you think is gross and vile
Makes us sing and dance and smile.
We like to live like that."

At the end of the song, Botticelli signaled for the feast to begin. The rats tossed a rotten apple core up into the sky. It exploded in midair, raining slimy pulp and seeds onto the roaring crowd. The younger rats dived on the putrid garbage. They crammed it into their mouths, slurping and slobbering, while their elders began singing all over again.

All except one, that is.

Roscuro stood motionless in the torchlight, watching.

"You're not dancing," came a low voice to his left.

Roscuro turned to see Botticelli in the shadows.

"Oh, I was," said Roscuro nervously.

"No, you weren't."

"Well . . . I'm just . . . watching."

"Well, that's not very grateful of you after I've taken you under my wing." Botticelli wrapped a long, bony arm around Roscuro's shoulders.

"Oh, I'm grateful," Roscuro insisted, a bit too eagerly. "Really! I am."

Botticelli leaned closer. "You miss something. Don't you?"

"Oh, no. I don't!" Roscuro protested, shrugging him off.

"There's nothing up there, Roscuro. Nothing at all."

"Oh, no. . . . I know that." Roscuro smiled sheepishly and backed away. "Absolutely. Nothing, of course. Uh . . . nothing."

He quickly turned and hurried off, as Botticelli watched him go.

"Nothing!" Roscuro called back.

A fat, lumpy rat named Smudge sidled up to Botticelli.

"That's a tough one," said Smudge. "You're not going to turn him, you're not."

"Oh, I don't know," said Botticelli, his red eyes still on Roscuro. He licked one of his long claws. "A rat is a rat. It doesn't really matter where you come from."

Roscuro ran away into the orange night, missing that "something" all the more. He wound his way through the throng of rats and slipped away from the crowd.

Heading in the other direction, Roscuro hurried past the crowded village. He climbed over bones and garbage toward the outskirts of town, where a stone wall marked the edge of the rat world. Roscuro followed the wall down to a corner, where he found what he'd been looking for.

Casting one last furtive glance over his shoulder, he squeezed into the wall's slim crevice. Inside, the space opened up into a small nook. Roscuro reached down and, with all his might, pulled back one of the bricks. He stepped into his private hiding place.

The passage was small, but from within it Roscuro could look up to see one faint, gray sliver of light. Roscuro let the light wash over him, drinking it in as if he needed it to live.

And maybe he did.

Then he just stared, hungrily, longingly. . . .

CHAPTER TWELVE

How to Be Afraid

In another part of the castle, someone else was also longing.

A thin ray of light filtered through the storeroom windowpane, and a small mouse gazed up at it, completely entranced.

Somehow, somewhere, there has to be someone more like me, Despereaux thought, looking out into the vast world beyond.

He was so absorbed, he did not notice the gang of mice watching him from the edge of the schoolyard, half a block away. They were once his friends. But lately, they'd begun to look differently upon the mouse who was so unlike them.

"He is so weird," one remarked.

"No kidding," said another. He mimicked Despereaux, *"Oh, that is so beautiful. I wonder what's out there."*

The others laughed at the imitation.

But Despereaux, still unaware he was being watched, continued to stare out the window. "That is *so* beautiful," he said softly. "I wonder what's *out* there."

Laughter exploded behind him. Despereaux turned just as the mice looked quickly away and whispered among themselves.

It's one thing to be different from everyone else. But when you *know* you're different and you can't do anything about it . . .

"Feb. 1: Doesn't scurry. . . . Feb. 3: Didn't cower.'"
Inside his office, the principal was reading

aloud from a lengthy report to Despereaux's parents.

"'*Didn't cower . . . Didn't cower . . . wouldn't scurry. . . .*'" the portly mouse murmured, skimming the rest of the teacher's comments. "Oh, here's one, *'Drew a picture of a cat on his notebook'*"

Lester swallowed hard. "A cat?"

"Oh, I can't imagine," said Antoinette.

"I'm afraid so," said the principal, nodding gravely. "Named it Fluffy."

"Oh, I had no idea . . ." Lester said. "I . . . oh . . ."

The principal handed Mr. and Mrs. Tilling the offending notebook. Despereaux's parents cringed. From the book's cover, a large tomcat smiled up at them.

Outside the principal's office, Despereaux sat waiting. The office door creaked open.

"Despereaux?" said the principal.

"Yes, sir?" Despereaux answered.

"Come in, please."

Despereaux sat between his parents. He was so tiny that the principal could see only two big ears sticking out from behind the pillbox desk.

"Despereaux," the principal said, "why do you think you're in school?"

"To learn?" Despereaux said, wondering if he'd been asked a trick question.

"To learn," said Lester. "Yes, good."

"Yes, that's good," Antoinette echoed.

"To learn what?" the principal demanded.

"To learn how to be a mouse, sir," Despereaux said.

"That is correct. And you can't be a mouse if you don't learn how to be afraid," the principal said. "Despereaux, there are so many wonderful things in life to be afraid of, if you just learn how scary they are."

"Yes, sir. I guess," said Despereaux, torn. "Yes, sir."

The principal turned his attention back to Lester and Antoinette. "How about his brother?" he asked.

"His brother? What about him?" Lester asked, alarmed.

"Yes. Is he, you know, timid?"

Lester and Antoinette exhaled in relief. "Oh, yes," they said at once. "Very timid. Timid as the day is long."

"Good." The principal nodded. "Because sometimes they just need to see the older ones do it. No one starts out afraid."

"Understood," said Lester.

"Of course," said his wife.

The meeting caused Lester and Antoinette a great deal of paw-wringing. Where had they gone wrong? they lamented. Surely one of them was to blame for their son's shameful lack of fear.

"You coddle that boy. That's the problem,"

Lester said to his wife as they walked across the school's checkered courtyard.

"No, no," Antoinette said.

"Yes, you do."

"No, no."

"Yes, you do. You've been doing it all along."

"But he is so little," Antoinette said. "I have had to help him."

"He is not going to be afraid unless you allow him to be afraid."

Antoinette pondered her husband's advice. Maybe he was right. Maybe it was time to let her baby discover fear. But *she* certainly wasn't going to be the one to help him. No, she would not even be able to watch.

"Furlough will teach him," Antoinette said decisively.

And so it was settled. Like it or not, Despereaux Tilling was going to learn how to be a mouse.

CHAPTER THIRTEEN

The Lesson

At his parents' demand, Furlough met Despereaux just inside he mousehole that led to the royal kitchen.

"Do what he does," Lester told Despereaux.

"And don't do anything he doesn't," added Antoinette.

"And if he's afraid of something—" Lester began.

"Then you need to be afraid of it, too," Antoinette said.

"Are you ready?" Furlough asked his little brother.

"Yeah," Despereaux answered, nodding. But he wasn't really paying attention. He was focused on the light from the royal kitchen beyond. The outside world of humans was much more interesting—and dangerous. He couldn't wait to explore it.

Despereaux hurried out in front of his brother. From inside the safety of the mouse-hole, Lester and Antoinette watched their sons creep into the kitchen.

It didn't take but a moment for André to spot the two mice—one cowering and the other unusually tiny, but bold. The small one didn't even flinch. Instead, he looked straight at the chef. André just stared sadly back at him.

"Come on, Despereaux! Hurry up!" Furlough said, dragging his brother away.

The pair scurried up the banister of a large staircase and through the castle's second floor until they found their destination.

Despereaux and Furlough entered a magnificent room.

The royal library took Despereaux's breath away. Faded sunlight streamed through a row of high windows to illuminate books, books, and more books. Shelves lined every wall from floor to ceiling, and each one was packed with books of all types and sizes. A long table stretched across the center of the room. Its surface was covered with tomes that lay open as if in the middle of being read. But of course, no one had read anything since the queen's death.

Despereaux gaped at the scenery as Furlough led him to a storybook and invited his brother to take a seat upon the first page.

"All right. Now you start nibbling right along that edge there," instructed Furlough, looking around nervously. "The glue is all right, but it's the pages that taste the best."

While Furlough talked, the words on the page stretched away from Despereaux like some strange and beautiful road.

"'Once upon a time,'" Despereaux read. He looked up at his brother. "That's great, isn't it? 'Upon' a time. And they don't even tell you what time that is yet. Like you have to find that out."

Furlough groaned. "You're not supposed to *read* it, Despereaux! You're supposed to eat it!"

Despereaux halfheartedly licked some glue along the spine.

"Good," Furlough said, turning to leave. "I'll come back in an hour."

Despereaux peeked at the tempting line of print behind him. Surely it wouldn't hurt to—

"And NO reading!" Furlough called from the doorway.

Despereaux jumped.

"It's a RULE!" Furlough shouted. And finally he was gone.

Despereaux glanced down at the ripped edge he was supposed to eat and tried not to look behind him at the page full of words.

But he couldn't stand it anymore. "Just one sentence," he said to himself.

The line of print ran away from him as he read:

Once upon a time, there lived a . . .

Despereaux walked across the page.

fair princess. Fairer than any in any other land.

Despereaux disappeared into the valley between the pages. A moment later, his head popped up between them.

"Hmm," he mused. "Fair . . ."

He ran out of the valley and across the page to continue reading:

She was locked up in a faraway castle, where she could see the world but never touch it.

"That seems awful," Despereaux said to himself. "To see the world, but never touch it." He read on:

She longed for a prince. A brave knight who would deliver her from all of this. Someone with courage and honor and decency.

Courage. Honor. Decency. The words seemed to lift from the page and swirl around Despereaux. The images these words evoked in his mind sprang to life before him.

Despereaux imagined a knight fighting in a fierce battle. Swords clashed. Hooves thundered. There was dust and shouting and trumpets.

But in a cruel and frightened world, men like this were scarce indeed. For it wasn't just courage that made a knight....

In Despereaux's mind, the brave knight charged toward a ferocious dragon and into the flames of its breath....

Though without the courage to fight for it, chivalry is useless.

Despereaux looked up in amazement.

His imaginary knight was now at a small farm outside the castle. A grateful peasant was thanking the knight for restoring his lands. The knight plucked a single red feather from his helmet and handed it to the man's daughter.

Then, without a word, the knight turned and rode off toward the horizon, a striking silhouette against the setting sun.

And it wasn't just chivalry, either — although without it, the battle would have no meaning.

At a round table, the knight dined with his friends in a great hall. Knights all, they were noble and regal. They laughed; they showed kindness; their word was true.

Despereaux kept reading.

They lived in a special world built on courage and chivalry and honor. They pledged their lives to one another. To fight for truth. To defend the weak. To seek justice. . . .

Despereaux read as much as he could until Furlough returned to get him. Then he thought of princesses and knights, honor and chivalry, the whole way home.

CHAPTER FOURTEEN

A Kiss from a Princess

Later, at a much smaller table, Despereaux's family gathered for dinner.

Theirs was nothing like the knights' great hall. The Tillings' dining room did not know such laughter and warmth. This was a "proper" family dinner.

"How was the library?" Lester asked his son, passing him a plate of cheese.

"Fine," said Despereaux.

"Spoil your appetite?" Lester asked.

"No," Despereaux said, thinking about the knight and the princess, courage and decency.

"Helped it, actually," he said. "Made me hungrier."

"Did you get started on a book?" asked Lester.

Despereaux nodded. "Devoured it," he said.

Lester looked over to Antoinette. *This just might be progress,* they thought.

"Good lad," Lester said.

Despereaux didn't respond. He was too busy waving his fork like a sword.

"Ha, ha!" he cried.

Did a book ever speak to you? Almost as if it were written for you? Despereaux couldn't wait to get back to the library. All that week, he returned to read more of the story.

Despereaux jumped back and forth across the pages. He had brought his fork with him, and he jabbed it into the air like a sword as he read.

The knight rode into battle. . . .

"Ha, ha!" Despereaux yelled, slaying an imaginary dragon.

He loved it all — every bit of it: the truth, the justice, the bravery, the sword fighting.

He lay on the page, then rolled over on to his back and stared up at the library's elaborate vaulted ceiling. He tried to picture what he'd just read.

The story said that the princess was a prisoner, but that wasn't totally true. Because she had hope. And whenever you have hope, you're never really anybody's prisoner.

Despereaux turned back to the page and studied an illustration of the golden-haired princess. She stood at the window of a tower, gazing out at her kingdom. The castle was huge, the sky was clear, and the princess was fair. Illustrated in lavish detail, she seemed to radiate light.

Despereaux read on.

"Someday my prince will come," said the *princess.*

"But how does she KNOW that?" Despereaux wondered aloud.

A soft sound interrupted his thoughts. A sad, sweet melody was drifting in from outside the library's door. Despereaux hopped off the book and ventured into the corridor of the castle.

There, the music grew louder. Someone was playing a guitar — the same mournful refrain over and over. Despereaux wandered down the large stone hallway toward the sound.

He followed the song to an enormous room. The room was spacious even to humans, but it was especially cavernous and grand to a mouse.

Tucked in a corner, a man sat, lost in a huge chair. It was the king, playing his guitar. He finished playing, sighed, and gazed up at a portrait of his dead queen.

That's when Despereaux noticed someone else in the room. Pea, too, was watching her father. But the king didn't seem to know she was there. It might be said that in his grief, the king had forgotten he had a daughter at all.

Princess Pea could stand it no longer. As the king began playing his sad and beautiful song all over again, she turned away from him and left the room.

In her chamber, Princess Pea stood at her window, alone, and stared out across the bleak countryside. A warm amber glow surrounded her. She was lovely. She looked almost like the princess from the storybook.

Tears filled her eyes. She sniffed.

"Why are you crying?" asked Despereaux.

Pea turned around, but she did not see anyone.

"Why are you crying?" Despereaux said, a bit louder.

Pea looked left, then right.

"Um . . . down here!" he called.

She looked down, and then she saw him. A small mouse with exceptionally large ears was standing on the arm of her chair.

"Aaah!" cried Pea. "Are you a rat?"

"No," Despereaux answered.

"What are you?" Pea asked. "A mouse?"

"I," Despereaux said, doffing his hat, "am a gentleman."

Pea smiled. She leaned in a little closer. "How do you do?" she asked.

"You're sad," said Despereaux.

"Yes," she said.

"Because you have 'longing,'"

Pea's eyes widened. "Yes!"

"But 'longing is just love waiting to be born,'" the little mouse explained.

"You're a strange little mouse," Pea said.

"Thank you," Despereaux said, smiling.

"Um . . . do you want some cheese?"

"No, thank you," Despereaux replied. "I have already eaten."

Pea smiled again and reached down to offer her hand. "Come on," she said.

Despereaux hesitated. Then he walked onto her outstretched palm. The princess lifted him up until he was right in front of her eyes, where she could get a closer look at him.

"Where did you hear about that? About 'longing'?" she asked.

"In a story."

"A story? About what?"

"About a princess—like you. Trapped in a castle—like this," Despereaux said.

"Oh, you're a smooth little mouse, aren't you?" Pea asked, raising an eyebrow. "I'll bet you tell that to all the princesses."

"I am sworn to tell the truth," Despereaux said. "It's a code of honor."

"Ah!" said the princess. "Not just a gentleman. An honorable gentleman."

Despereaux bowed slightly.

"Well, then, how does this story end—with the princess who is locked in a castle?"

"I don't know," said Despereaux, slightly embarrassed. "I haven't finished it yet."

"I'd love to know," Pea said. She set Despereaux down and looked out the window.

"Oh, I wish it would *rain*. I wish there were soup again. I even wish there were rats!" Pea looked down at Despereaux. "Will you promise me something? Will you promise to finish your story and tell me how it ends?"

"Yes," Despereaux promised. "It will be my quest."

"Your 'quest'?" Pea said. "You are a very brave mouse." And with that, the princess leaned forward and did something extraordinary.

She kissed her finger and touched it to his nose. Sweetly, softly. "Thank you, my good gentleman," she said.

If a mouse could blush, Despereaux would have been scarlet. He slid down the tablecloth and gazed up at Pea's smiling face.

A kiss. A kiss. A kiss from a princess!

This was all Despereaux could think as he waved good-bye to Pea. Just the very thought of her kiss sent him floating out of her room and flying down the marble banister.

"Ah, ahhhhhh!" Despereaux cried.

CHAPTER FIFTEEN

Miggery Sow

There are all kinds of princesses. Some are born that way. Some marry into it. And some are destined to be princesses only in their own minds.

No one would mistake Miggery Sow for a princess. Certainly not while she was on her hands and knees scrubbing the marble floor of the Great Hall.

Even when not on all fours, Mig, as she was called, bore an unfortunate resemblance to a pig. Her nose turned up, her cheeks puffed out, and her body was more than a little porcine.

Mig scoured the floor with a course brush. Back and forth. Back and forth. It was hard, tedious work. But every now and then, Mig took a break and gazed up at the top of the hall's long, long staircase.

Above the stairs, a portrait of Princess Pea adorned the wall. The painted Pea looked down upon the palace in all her fairy-tale loveliness.

Pretty princess, Mig thought dreamily, imagining herself in such a portrait. But when she went back to scrubbing, all Mig saw was her own sad face reflected in the marble floor.

Miggery Sow wasn't born into royalty. And who'd marry her? But at one time or another, almost every little girl longs to be a princess.

Characters and Scenes from the Movie

the king

Princess Pea

the queen

The Tilling family and the doctor gather around baby Despereaux's crib.

Despereaux discovers a book in the royal library.

Despereaux steals cheese from a mousetrap.

Despereaux meets Princess Pea.

Cooks make soup in the royal kitchen.

Boldo and Despereaux set off to rescue Pea.

The Mouse Council condemns Despereaux to the dungeon.

In the deepest, darkest corner of

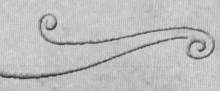

the dungeon, the rats dance and sing.

Roscuro

Not so long ago, a girl had slogged through the mud, scattering feed to a throng of pigs. She wiped her nose, smearing mud across her face.

The little girl lived in squalor, on a pig farm with a front yard full of slop. But in the distance a castle glowed with a dazzling light, and the girl was comforted by the sight of it.

"I'm gonna live right there," the girl said, pointing out the castle to one of her pigs.

The pig snorted.

"Right up there near the tippy top," she said.

"AH, QUIT YOUR DAYDREAMING!" a man covered in slop screamed in the girl's ear.

The daydreaming girl was Miggery Sow, and the slop-covered man was her uncle Ned.

Uncle Ned screamed loud—and often. He screamed so loud that his words began to sound like a shrill ringing in Mig's head. And he screamed so often that soon Mig didn't even hear the ringing anymore. Instead a soft, angelic note echoed in her own imagination.

"FEED THOSE SWINE!" Uncle Ned yelled.

"Yes, I know," said Mig, still staring at the castle. "It's going to be ALL mine."

"No, you deaf little urchin. I said, FEED THOSE SWINE!"

Miggery Sow had been shoveling slop for as long as she could remember. Her uncle Ned had put a shovel in her hand from the minute she could hold one. She didn't mind too much, she got on quite nicely with the pigs.

Pigs could be counted on. Pigs did not scream. Plus they were excellent listeners. Mig plopped down in the muck, and the swine gathered around, nuzzling her as she spoke.

"That's right," Mig told them. "I'm gonna have a special room just for me dresses an' another whole closet just for me knickers."

In fact, Miggery Sow could see her future very clearly. She could see the tiara, the fancy dresses, the maids-in-waiting. And when things got really bad around the farm, she could see the moment when she would finally be delivered from it all.

As the years passed, Mig only grew more convinced that she was destined to reside in the castle. Even as she herded the hogs into their sty for the umpteenth time.

"Not long now," Mig told them. "I promise you that."

So there she was, getting the last hog in the sty, when she noticed a visitor. Uncle Ned was talking to a man she'd never seen before. Mig wiped some slop from her forehead (accidentally wiping more slop onto it) and listened closely.

"Twenty for the big ones, fifteen for the sow, and twelve for the girl," the man said.

"Fifteen for the girl," countered Ned. "Same as the sow."

Before she knew it, Mig was being carried away, along with the pigs, on the back of the man's oxcart (although it was difficult to tell Mig and the pigs apart, all squished together as they were).

The cart pulled her through the broken-down gate of Uncle Ned's slop-filled yard and headed for that glorious castle in the distance.

"I told ya," Mig told her pigs. "I told ya I'd make it to the castle. Oooo-yeeee!"

So sometimes it doesn't take much for your dreams to come true. You just have to be able to see it that way.

From the back of the cart, Mig took one last look at the farm. She tried to straighten her hair and wipe the muck off her face (accidentally wiping more muck onto it) to make a good impression at the castle.

And now, there she was.

Mig sat on her knees and looked down at the tired, dirty face reflected in the marble floor. *Yep,* she said to herself, *I'm livin' in the castle, all right.*

Then Miggery Sow snorted and went back to work.

CHAPTER SIXTEEN

A Mouse in Love

Despereaux danced, flipped, and swooned all the way from Pea's bedroom to his own.

Furlough waited for him at home. He'd wanted to hear more about how Despereaux had nibbled the page. And how it had been quite tasty, too, with a fine, snappy crunch. But Furlough heard something else entirely.

"She was beautiful," said Despereaux. "Like an *angel*."

"You are crazy," said Furlough.

"And she *smelled* so amazing," Despereaux continued. "Like a garden."

"Despereaux, you can't talk to a *human*! That's the worst thing you can do!" Furlough said, throwing his paws up into the air.

"No, it's the best thing I ever did."

"They'll throw you in the dungeon. You'll get eaten by rats!"

"It would be worth it," said Despereaux fiercely. "They could tear at my flesh." He fell back upon his matchbox bunk bed and stared at the ceiling, lost in his own romantic tale.

"Oh, this is bad," said Furlough.

"And when she held me in her hand, it was so soft. Like floating on a pillow."

"You know what? I am worried about you."

"That's the point, Furlough. Don't worry! There's nothing to be afraid of!"

"*Quiet!*" Furlough pleaded. "They'll *hear* you!"

"C'mon. Just try it," said Despereaux. "Just for a second. Just try to be brave."

At the sound of the word "brave," Furlough hunched into a small, shivering ball.

"And *stop cowering*!" said Despereaux, which only made Furlough curl up tighter and cover his face with his paws.

Furlough was known to have above-average cowering abilities. But what he heard next made him cower to his utmost potential. From the doorway came a sudden and very angry voice.

"What's going on in here?" the voice demanded.

The mice jumped and turned to see their father.

"What's all this talk about princesses and b-b-bravery?" Lester asked.

Despereaux and the cowering Furlough looked at each other. What could they say? Lester Tilling had heard every word.

"Furlough, I want to see you. In my study," ordered Lester. "Right now!"

In the study, Furlough spoke to his parents. His words caused them to twitter and tremble. Lester paced back and forth, nodding occasionally and cringing often. But Furlough's last comment caused his father stop in his tracks.

"Are you sure?" Lester asked.

"That is what he said," answered Furlough.

"A real human?"

"A princess," Furlough said, hiding behind shaky paws.

"We need to tell them. We need to tell the Mouse Council."

"But they'll . . ." Antoinette said, unable to finish.

"This is bad," said Lester. "This is very bad. If they find out . . . If they find out that they *didn't* find out . . . Oh! Then they'll find out that it was me who . . . oh, no!"

"But they will send him to the dungeon!" cried Antoinette.

"He'll get eaten by rats!" Furlough added hysterically.

"Not if we beg. If we really beg," said Lester. "And show them that he's changed. That he's afraid. That he's afraid and he's turned into a real *mouse* and . . ."

Furlough and Antoinette quivered with dread, afraid to watch what Lester was about to do next.

"Despereaux!" Lester called.

The Tilling house was silent.

"Where is he?" Lester asked.

Despereaux was not at home. Despereaux was, at that very moment, running back toward the mousehole, toward the princess and light and adventure.

While, not so far away, someone watched the mouse flee.

If only the mayor had not seen Despereaux leave, the next part of this story might have turned out quite differently.

CHAPTER SEVENTEEN

A Man or a Mouse?

Of course, destiny is a funny thing. We go out to meet it, sometimes even when we don't know that we are.

A wide-open page spread out before Despereaux like a vast land. Its first line of print was a road that promised adventure. The mouse traveled over the landscape, reading as he walked.

The storybook knight galloped across the countryside toward a castle in the distance. The fair princess was still waiting by her window.

The knight thundered toward her. He stormed across the drawbridge and into the castle courtyard. He flew off the saddle, drew his sword, and bravely made his way toward the princess.

In her chambers, the princess turned as the valiant knight burst through the door. Their eyes met. Neither moved for a moment. Then they ran toward each other, and—

"Despereaux Tilling!"

Only this voice was not soft and light like that of a storybook princess. This voice was cold and brittle and quite real. Despereaux wheeled around.

Three elderly mice, led by the mayor, stood on the page. The members of the Mouse Council looked down upon Despereaux with scornful, beady eyes.

The mayor looked gravely from the mouse to the book.

"How long have you been working on this book?" he asked, inspecting its spine.

"Um . . . a week," Despereaux answered.

The mayor frowned at the abundance of perfectly good glue still remaining. "A week? You've hardly cracked it."

"Well . . . I was . . . I just want to see how it ends," Despereaux said truthfully.

This, as you might have guessed, was the wrong answer.

Back in the mouse world, a huge crowd was forming. News of a Mouse Council arrest spread quickly. Mice ran from their homes and swarmed the town square. They all clamored just inside the mousehole to get a better look at the prisoner about to enter. When he arrived, mice had to stand on park benches to catch a glimpse of him. The prisoner was so small. It was nearly impossible to see him among the council escorts and two burly guards. The spectators pointed and whispered the captured mouse's name.

You see, Despereaux Tilling was no longer an anonymous mouse, free to stare out the window and daydream. He was now a mouse accused of — and about to be tried for — unspeakable crimes.

In no time at all, Despereaux was seated in the Mouse Council courthouse.

Fashioned out of a grand silver humidor, the courthouse was designed to make a mouse feel small. Polished walls went on forever and the sky-high ceiling was decorated with the ornate seal of the cigar company.

And to ensure that a mouse felt smaller still, the Mouse Council sat at a long table that loomed high above the accused.

At the head of the table, the mayor recited Despereaux's crimes. "Refused training as a mouse, refused to respect the will and guidance of elder mice, repeatedly engaged in bold and 'unmeek' behavior, triggered, willfully, not less than seventeen mousetraps."

Here, the mayor paused dramatically while

the audience murmured. Despereaux smiled slightly to himself.

"Had personal contact with — with —" The mayor paused again. "With a human being."

The crowd gasped.

"Despereaux Tilling," the mayor said, "are these charges true?"

"Yes . . . I think so," Despereaux said, and then, trying to be helpful, added, "But I lost track of how many mousetraps."

"Do you understand the penalty for associating or conversing with a human being?" the mayor asked, his voice thundering down upon the little mouse.

Now where, you might be wondering, were Mr. and Mrs. Tilling seated during this inquisition? Lester and Antoinette were at home, too overcome with worry to watch.

By the living-room window, Lester cowered and rocked, cowered and rocked, with his wife beside him.

"Isn't there something you can do?" Antoinette asked, looking back toward the courthouse in agony.

"Antoinette, stop," said Lester, wringing his paws. "Stop that. You have to trust them. They're the council. They're the council 'cause, 'cause . . . they're the council."

CHAPTER EIGHTEEN

The Threadmaster

"Is there anything you wish to say in your defense?" the mayor asked Despereaux.

The mouse glanced around the courtroom. For perhaps the first time in his life, Despereaux felt small — and afraid.

"Well, it was a very good story and . . ." he said, "she was a very beautiful princess."

"So you admit that you had contact with a human being?"

"Yes," Despereaux said, smiling at the memory of Pea's kiss. "I did."

The audacity of his last statement set off a whole new round of murmurs. The judges huddled to consult among themselves at once.

Their verdict came swiftly.

"Despereaux Tilling," said the mayor, "the judgment of this court is not an easy one, but it is clear. Our laws are here to protect us and our way of life. And when one of our citizens strays from that way of life, he becomes a threat to us all.

"It's an easy question: Are you a man, or are you a mouse? And your actions have told us that you have a great deal of trouble being a mouse.

"It is the judgment of this court," the mayor continued, "that you should be banished from these walls forever!

"You shall be remanded into the custody of Hovis the Threadmaster, who will prepare you for your descent into the unknown world that lies beneath us.

"You shall be exiled — alone — into the dungeons of Dor, from which no mouse and no light has ever escaped."

For once, the courtroom was stunned into silence.

"Is there anything you wish to say to clear your conscience or your soul?" the mayor asked Despereaux.

"I don't think so," he replied.

"Very well," said the mayor.

And that, as they say, was that. There was no time for good-byes. And there wasn't anyone there to say good-bye to, anyway. Despereaux had to leave immediately.

Hovis the Threadmaster was waiting.

Pa-ruum, pa-ruum, pa-ruum.

A slow and steady drumbeat accompanied Despereaux's march from the courthouse.

The town square was jammed with mice.

It had been a long time since a mouse was exiled, and at this rate, who knew when the next one would be?

Mouse guards escorted Despereaux through the dense mob. The other mice gasped and cut a wide path for him as he passed. A few hooted and jeered.

Hidden among the crowd, Lester and Antoinette Tilling watched, too.

"Despereaux!" Antoinette cried.

"Shhh," said Lester.

"My baby!" she wailed.

"Qu-quiet, dear," whispered Lester. "There's nothing to be done."

Despereaux's parents could only watch as their son was led toward the back of the mouse village. He was entering the darkest part of the mouse world, where few lived and fewer traveled (certainly no respectable mouse). The streets dwindled into dusty alleys, and the buildings turned back into what they once were: broken urns, rotting shoes, and other trash.

At the edge of this neglected part of town, the crowd fell away. No one was willing to tread any closer to either the darkness or the fearsome-looking mouse who led the prisoner.

The guards thrust Despereaux at Hovis the Threadmaster, then turned and ran away as fast as they could.

Despereaux looked up at the threadmaster, who was shrouded in a long leather coat and a black hood that hid his face. He was an alarmingly large mouse, especially next to his tiny prisoner.

Hovis turned and led the mouse across a narrow bridge. At the end, they came to the door of an upside-down glass dome, the threadmaster's lair. Hovis motioned abruptly for Despereaux to enter.

In the distance, the crowd could barely watch.

Despereaux stepped into the dome. Inside was an old, broken sewing box. The lair was gloomy and cramped. In every direction, spools and spools of thread rose above the mouse in frightening towers. To Despereaux, the thread looked as thick as rope. He shivered, knowing it was all used for one sinister purpose.

"Stand there," Hovis said, pointing to the top of a spool of thread. He seemed to study Despereaux for a moment. Then he selected a spool of red thread and pulled out a couple of lengths.

"Red?" Despereaux asked.

Hovis took a sharp knife from his belt. "So they tell me," he said, swiftly cutting the thread.

Despereaux looked closer at the large mouse. Hovis had not selected the thread by sight, but touch. The threadmaster was blind.

In one fluid movement, Hovis expertly

tied the thread tightly around Despereaux's waist, so that its length streamed behind.

"So you're the 'brave' one," Hovis said.

"I guess," said Despereaux.

Hovis finished the knot. "That's good. It'll carry well down there."

Despereaux looked at the long scarlet string that followed him.

"Wear it proudly," said the large mouse. "There's no shame."

Despereaux nodded.

"It's time," said the threadmaster.

CHAPTER NINETEEN

In the Dungeon

Despereaux emerged from Hovis's lair with the red thread following him like a trail of blood.

Far behind them, the crowd shivered at the sight.

"It's all right," Hovis said. "They're too scared to come down here."

Despereaux followed Hovis into the darkness. They traveled along the twists and turns of a dirty path. The farther they walked into this no-mouse's-land, the higher the rubbish soared. The stinky piles cast eerie shadows over their heads.

At last, Hovis stopped at a spot in the floor where a rusted grate covered a drain. It looked like the same grate Despereaux had once eagerly peered into. The same endless blackness. The same detestable stench. But to Despereaux, it looked blacker and smelled more heinous now.

"In there?" asked Despereaux.

"I'm afraid so," said Hovis, motioning for Despereaux to stand on a ledge overhanging the grate. On the ledge was a strange mechanism. A tripod of three tall wooden poles held a spool of red thread horizontally. The long end of the thread dangled from the contraption, spilling onto the ledge and down a long plank, into the grate below.

Despereaux stepped onto the ledge. He peered down into the drainpipe. It was pitch-black within, and damp.

"Courage, right?" said Hovis, picking up the thread and tying it to Despereaux's waist.

"And truth," said Despereaux. "And honor."

"Good. But especially courage."

Despereaux hesitated, as if digesting the words.

"I'm ready," he said at last.

Hovis placed a paw on the mechanism's lever. Then, ever so slowly, he began to lower Despereaux through the grate.

"All right, then you need to—" Hovis began.

The threadmaster's voice was drowned out by a whirring sound, which was followed by a high-pitched whine. Despereaux had already jumped. The thread spooled away from Hovis with a scream.

Despereaux hurtled into the mouth of the dungeon. His arms flew out at his sides. The wind buffeted his face and flapped the corners of his hat. He was free-falling into the abyss, and there was no sign of stopping or slowing down. The little mouse felt as heavy as a rock.

At this point, it must be said that the mouse was not scared. He was terrified.

Then, bit by bit, his large ears slowed his descent, until he was less like a rock and more like a leaf. The dark green, murky water of the rat world began to swim toward him. The mouse was nearly there.

Somehow, within this blackness, a sliver of faint light caught his eye. Something shone from the side of the shaft.

Despereaux saw the opening of light in the wall below him. And as he drifted past, his paw shot up to grab it. He scrambled into a small passageway, a vent in the sewer.

With his feet on solid ground, the mouse took a deep breath. He untied the red thread from his waist, left it behind, and walked cautiously forward into the dim light.

Despereaux moved slowly, feeling his

way. Something creaked beneath his feet. Despereaux stopped. He looked down. He took a step. And suddenly, he was falling again.

Thunk, thunk, thunk — the mouse tumbled down a staircase and slammed onto a cold, slimy floor. Despereaux took a deep breath, wheezed, and moved gingerly forward.

He came face to face with a human skull. The mouse stifled a scream. He froze.

Courage, he told himself, remembering the threadmaster's words.

Despereaux took a breath and continued on through the darkened corridor.

He tried not to listen to the dungeon's mysterious sounds: the scratching, gnawing, and moans of pain. He tried not to look at cell door after cell door, all bolted shut with only a tiny slit for a window.

Most of all, the mouse tried not to think about who — or how many — followed him as he headed into the void.

CHAPTER TWENTY

Gregory the Jailer

Gregory the jailer sat on his stool in a pool of light cast from a single oil lamp. His huge ring of keys hung at his side. Rats crawled all over him, but Gregory hardly noticed. He was snoring.

"Hello?" Despereaux called into the darkness. "Hello?"

Gregory woke with a jump.

"Let's go, let's go . . . on the double," came a whisper. It was Smudge, ordering the rats off of Gregory. They raced out of sight and hid behind a grate in the wall.

"Who is that? Who goes there?" Gregory asked, holding his lamp aloft. "Who is that?"

"Despereaux Tilling," said a tiny voice in the darkness.

Gregory lowered the lamp toward the sound. "Are ye a man, or are ye a mouse?"

"I . . ." said Despereaux shakily, "am a gentleman."

Gregory crept closer with the oil lamp until its light landed upon two ears. Despereaux stood as tall as he could — almost a full three inches. Gregory leaned over to inspect his small visitor. He reached down and snatched him up in a large, rough hand and squeezed the little mouse.

Despereaux's cheeks turned bright red. Then his ears turned purple. He thought he was going to faint.

Gregory squinted to see him. "And what makes ye think yer a 'gentleman'?"

"A code of honor," Despereaux said, with

the cough of a mouse who is being choked to death.

"HARRRRR, yer a strange little mouse. And where do you find this 'code of honor'?"

"In a story," said the mouse, "a legend that I read."

Across the room, several little red eyes peered out from the darkness.

"It's a mouse!" said a low voice.

"Shh," said Smudge. "Quiet, lads. Patience."

"Fine," said Gregory to the mouse. "Tell me about this 'legend' of yours. I could do with a good story right now."

Despereaux tried as best as he could to tell the story, while still being squeezed in Gregory's giant hand. "Well . . . it's about a princess . . . and a knight," he said with a wheeze. "And his quest to save her honor—"

"Ahh. It was the princess that took away my soup!" Gregory said, squeezing the mouse tighter in his anger.

"She didn't take it," Despereaux said, coughing louder. "In fact, she misses it, too."

The rats listened in the darkness. But one face poked out from the shadows. Roscuro hung on Despereaux's every word.

"How do you know all this?" Gregory asked.

"I've seen her," Despereaux replied.

"Seen her."

"I've talked to her," Despereaux said.

"Talked to her."

"That's why they sent me down here."

"And what did this princess tell you when you had your royal 'audience'?" Gregory asked with a nasty laugh. "Oh, you must be a 'royal' mouse. Is that it?"

"She told me that she missed the soup and the rain and most of all, the sunlight," said Despereaux.

Roscuro's eyes widened, and Gregory's smirk faded. Even in the weak lamplight, the pain etched across the jailer's face was visible.

"Well, I don't want to hear your little stories about princesses and sunshine. Go tell them to the rats!" Gregory the jailer flung the mouse across the room.

Despereaux bashed against the wall. He lay dazed on the dungeon floor.

Smudge stepped out of the shadows and pointed to the new arrival. "All right, boys. Get that mouse!"

Despereaux groaned and stirred slightly. When he opened his eyes again, he was sure he was seeing stars. A million little red dots glowed in the darkness.

By the time the mouse's eyes adjusted, it was too late. The rat faces were already closing in on him—a wall of crazed, angry eyes and drooling, sharp fangs.

The rats scratched, gnawed, and licked their lips, imagining how the little mouse tasted.

Only one rat hung back as the hungry pack engulfed Despereaux.

CHAPTER TWENTY-ONE

Captured

The next thing he knew, Despereaux was tumbling out of a pipe onto a stone floor.

He was still in the dungeon. He knew this not because he could see the rats, but because he could *hear* them.

"MOUSE! MOUSE! MOUSE! MOUSE!" the voices chanted.

Despereaux looked straight up, raising his head toward the sound.

Hundreds of bloodthirsty rats leaned out over the top of the tall walls that encircled him. They peered down at their new victim far below, and their fangs dripped in hunger.

Despereaux looked around for an exit, but he was trapped. He found himself locked in some sort of arena, and whatever was about to happen was causing the rats above him to smack their chops in anticipation.

"Ha, ha!" Botticelli laughed wickedly. Like a Roman emperor, he occupied the prized position in the center of the coliseum. He sat in the royal box, where only a few chosen rats were allowed to join him.

"Good crowd, ain't it, sir?" asked Smudge.

"Yes, it is. Quite," said Botticelli as another rat slipped into the seat next to him.

"Ah, Roscuro," said Botticelli. "I'm glad you could make it. I thought you didn't like the arena."

"Oh . . . uh . . . oh, no," said Roscuro. "It's an honor, sir."

"Good. Well, enjoy," said Botticelli. "Let the games begin."

The shouts grew steadily louder as Despereaux's head began to clear.

"MOUSE! MOUSE! MOUSE! MOUSE!"

Botticelli stood and raised a long arm to quiet the frenzied crowd. At his command, the rats immediately silenced. He turned expectantly to the audience.

It was time.

Botticelli nodded. A moment later, a door opened in the arena. A giant, snarling tomcat entered. The crowd roared.

Despereaux did not dare to look at the beast, but he smelled it. And he heard it. The cat hissed, and Despereaux jumped into the air. The crowd burst into laughter as Despereaux frantically sprinted along the arena's walls, scrambling to find a way out.

The cat scratched at a post, not yet noticing Despereaux. From the top of the wall, a rat threw a ball of wool into the arena to divert the cat's attention. The ball bounced and rolled. The cat's eyes followed the ball's path—straight to the feet of the shaking little mouse.

The tomcat moved toward Despereaux and swiped at him with its giant paw. Despereaux leaped out of the way as five sharp claws sliced though the air where he'd just been standing. The cat snarled and began to pounce, but it was stopped short. A chain attached to its collar was the only thing keeping the cat from tearing the mouse to pieces. The cat strained, struggling to reach Despereaux.

Botticelli signaled again: this time, for the chain to be loosened.

The cat advanced on Despereaux and hissed loudly into the mouse's large ears. Despereaux ran through the cat's legs. The chase was on. The cat followed Despereaux around and around the arena.

It wasn't long before the mouse was cornered. Despereaux was pinned against the wall. The cat raised its paw, ready to strike for the last time.

The rats were on the edge of their seats. They were waiting for the signal from Botticelli. Any second now. . . .

Botticelli rose and moved to lower his thumb.

"WAIT!" a voice cried. "Can I have him?"

Botticelli turned to the rat seated next to him.

"Can I have this one?" Roscuro asked. "Please?"

"What?" asked Botticelli, surprised.

"I just . . ." Roscuro said. "That one looks so tasty."

"Well, this is progress," said Botticelli with an icy smile. "Perhaps we're starting to leave the past behind us. Enjoy, my friend! Don't leave a morsel."

"Oh, I—I—I won't," promised Roscuro.

The enraged cat was so close to Despereaux that the mouse could count its many jagged teeth and smell its hot, reeking breath blasting down upon his head.

The cat licked its lips, ready to eat.

From behind the rail, Botticelli raised his paw into the air. At the new signal, a rat reeled the chain in and dragged the surprised cat away. The crowd let out a huge groan of disappointment.

Then Botticelli, like a proud father, placed a clawed paw on Roscuro's shoulder and led him through the box to retrieve his gift.

CHAPTER TWENTY-TWO

A Gentleman

The other rats hauled Despereaux into the crowded street and thrust him at Roscuro's feet.

Roscuro yanked Despereaux upright. "C'mon!" the rat said loudly, shoving the mouse through the crowd. "Let's go, buster!"

Roscuro's request for his own mouse had suddenly made him a rat among rats. The others patted him on the back. They whooped as he tugged on the mouse's leash. And they urged Roscuro to finish every savory bone.

"That's it, that's it. Keep moving," Roscuro ordered Despereaux, to the amusement of the others. Then the rat bent down toward the mouse to whisper, "It's OK. Keep walking."

Roscuro pulled his catch around a corner, and the two walked until they were alone on a side street.

The mouse looked up at his captor in terror.

Despereaux was faced with a question that no mouse wants to answer. Was it worse to be trapped in a box with a cat—or alone with a rat in a dark alley?

Roscuro leaned in close to Despereaux's face. "Right up there," he whispered. "Keep walking."

The rat glanced over his shoulder at the desolate street. Then, quickly, he pulled Despereaux into the narrow gap in the wall.

Within the crevice, Roscuro untied the mouse. Despereaux watched as the rat pulled a brick from the wall to open up a passage and motioned for the mouse to enter.

Despereaux hesitated. His heart pounded in panic. But what could he do? He squeezed inside.

Within Roscuro's hiding place, a faint light placed a soothing kiss upon the frightened mouse.

"Oh. . . ." said Despereaux.

"See that? Light," Roscuro said. "Real light."

Despereaux looked up.

"It's mine," said the rat. "You can share it."

Despereaux glanced at the rat who was supposed to eat him.

"It isn't much," said Roscuro. "But there isn't much light anywhere since everything turned gray."

The mouse raised his head toward the light again. It was a slight trickle, but it warmed him to the bone.

"You're not going to eat me?" Despereaux asked the rat.

"No," said Roscuro. "I don't eat mice."

"Then what do you eat?"

"Crumbs, when I can find them."

"So you are a gentleman?" asked Despereaux.

Roscuro studied the mouse. When everyone calls you a rat, *gentleman* is a powerful word.

"Tell me that story," said Roscuro. "About the princess."

Despereaux looked embarrassed.

"Tell me what she looked like," said Roscuro.

"Well, she was . . ."

"Was she . . . angry?" Roscuro asked.

"No, not at all," Despereaux said. "Her heart was full of longing."

"What's longing?" asked the rat.

And that's how a friendship was born.

Over the next few weeks, Despereaux told Roscuro everything he knew about loyalty and honor and chivalry and courage. He told him about the princess and where her longing came from: that she missed the rain and the soup and even the rats.

"Even the rats?" Roscuro asked.

Despereaux told him about the code of honor. About his noble quest. About duty and loyalty.

And there — in the darkness of the cellar — two "knights" pledged devotion to a princess who was trapped inside a castle — trapped in a life full of pain and longing, even if no one could tell. Because sometimes what someone looks like on the outside has nothing to do with what they're feeling on the inside.

CHAPTER TWENTY-THREE

Mig's Punishment

In Pea's chamber, two pudgy hands removed the princess's jeweled tiara from its place on the dressing table. The tiara's diamonds glittered as it was raised into the air and carried across the room.

"Your crown, ma'am," said Miggery Sow.

"I don't want it today," said Pea. She sat by the window, staring out endlessly at her mother's grave.

"But it's beautiful, ma'am," Mig said, stroking the diamonds. The jewels shone brilliantly, especially when held next to Mig's dreary uniform.

"I know," said Pea. "But I don't want it."

"You look so pretty in it, ma'am. Like a princess."

"I know," said Pea, casting Mig an exasperated look. "I *am* the princess."

"Oh, I know, ma'am," said Mig, placing the tiara upon Pea's head. "But such a fine princess with the little pretty, glittery—"

"I don't want it. All right, Mig?" Pea snapped, backing away.

Miggery Sow's puffy cheeks reddened. "Very well, ma'am."

"Please take it away," Pea commanded.

Mig turned and carried the tiara back to Pea's dressing table. "Hmph," she grunted. If *she* was the pretty princess, she would wear the little glittery tiara, Mig thought. She would wear it every day, even to bed.

Mig set the tiara down, and then she did something sneaky. She slid open the dressing table's drawer. Inside, Pea's jeweled comb sparkled with light.

The comb was a shiny, pretty thing. And it was swiftly moved from the drawer of Pea's dressing table to the pocket of Mig's drab housecoat.

As you might expect, the room of a servant girl is very different from the room of a princess. Mig's room was smaller than Pea's closet, and it didn't have a fancy bed. But sometimes, one's imagination can do amazing things.

The servant girl sat alone in front of a cracked mirror and combed her greasy hair.

"Princess? Who's the princess? I'm a princess," said Mig, and then trying it another way, "I'm the *princess.*"

She set Pea's jeweled comb down upon her vanity, which was nothing more than on old box. But to Mig, it was the princess's dressing table. And every day, it *did* begin to look more and more like it, adorned as it was with the many items swiped from the princess's chambers.

"My comb. My hat. My gloves. My shoes. My pretty powder on me pretty princess face. . . ."

Mig looked up into the mirror again to suddenly see a pinched and sour face reflected next to her own.

"An' what do you think you're doin'?" Louise said, scowling behind her.

Mig spun around to face the head maid.

"Where did you get all this?" Louise asked. "I just borrowed it, ma'am," said Mig.

"*Borrowed* it?"

"I was gonna put 'em all back. . . ."

"See that you do!" said Louise, snatching Pea's tiara. "And you can spend the whole week taking slop down into the dungeon for your little . . . escapades."

Louise turned on her heel and stormed out of the servant girl's room. Her last word echoed in the hallway, loud enough for even Mig to hear.

"Princess!" she scoffed.

CHAPTER TWENTY-FOUR

The Rat's Quest

Miggery Sow creaked open the dungeon door.

A horrendous stench greeted her. But Mig's sense of smell was as bad as her hearing, and after living with the pigs, she had developed a formidable tolerance for stink.

Mig carefully carried a tray of food down the steep staircase. The stairway was darker than dark, too dark to see if she was holding the tray upright, too dark to see anything—

the tray, the steps, or even the pig nose in front of her face.

"Gor!" Mig said. "*She's* the princess. An' now I have to carry the sloppy, gloppy, stinky stew down in the damp, dark, dingy . . ." She blinked in the dark. "A person could get lost forever down—"

Mig stopped.

She was lost.

Gregory the jailer sat in his small circle of light. He looked up at the tray of gruel as it headed toward him with Mig behind it.

"Din-din!" called Mig.

"Slop," Gregory corrected her.

Miggery stopped.

"No, don't *stop!*" Gregory said. "I said *slop*." He waved the girl over, and she brought him his meal.

"How am I s'posed to eat this swill?" he

demanded. He looked at the bowl in disgust and flung it away.

"GOR! STOP THAT!" Mig yelled. "I don't have to be puttin' up with all this. I serve the princess."

"Ha! Right," said Gregory. "You serve the princess! That's a bit o' laugh, isn't it?"

"I do," Mig insisted. "I brings her tea an'—"

"Well, I don't want to hear it," Gregory said, cutting her off. "Had me own little princess once and now I don't."

"Gor! You had a *princess*?"

"Yeah," Gregory answered wistfully. "Every dad's got a princess . . . till he stops bein' a dad, of course."

Gregory turned from her and looked into the shadows.

"Oh," said Mig. "Well, I got a real one. An' she's got a tiara, and fancy robes, an' shiny bits all over every frock in her closet. An' I get to see her *every single day*."

Now, at this point, Gregory was well past

listening to Mig. He was lost in his own thoughts of regret and longing. But there was someone who was listening. Very closely.

In the shadows, Roscuro listened to Mig's every word.

When Roscuro returned to Despereaux in the hiding place, he was a different rat. He was a rat with a quest.

"What kind of a quest?" Despereaux asked him.

"To right a terrible wrong," said Roscuro. Standing in the shaft of light, the rat seemed taller, more powerful.

"But who did you wrong?" Despereaux asked.

Roscuro looked back at him, took a deep breath, and glanced up at the light. After a moment, he motioned the mouse over.

"OK," Roscuro whispered. "Do you know how they banished the rats?"

"Sure. . . . Yes," said Despereaux.

"Well, it wasn't *all* the rats they were mad at. It was because of one rat in particular."

Roscuro stared straight at Despereaux, but did not say a word.

After a moment, Despereaux got it. "You?" he whispered.

"Mmm-hmm," Roscuro said, nodding. "If—if I could just tell her I'm sorry. That I'm, you know, I'm *really* sorry. And that I didn't mean for any of this to happen. If she could just hear me say it, you know. Hear my voice. . . . She would know how much I meant it."

The mouse nodded and placed a small paw on his friend's shoulder. "That is a very noble quest indeed," Despereaux said solemnly.

So in a chink of a dungeon wall, under a precious light, a rat and a mouse planned a quest.

It was fortunate for them that Miggery Sow still could not see when she returned up the dark staircase. It was good luck indeed that she could not see the steps or the pig nose in front of her face — or most especially — the tray of slop.

Because on the tray, barely hidden under a napkin, a rat face peeked out of the shadows.

CHAPTER TWENTY-FIVE

A Crooked Heart

Princess Pea was in her usual place by the window, staring out over the bleak, gray landscape, when she heard a voice.

"Your — Your Highness?" the rat asked. He stood behind a bottle of perfume on her dressing table.

Pea turned toward the sound.

"Your *Highness*," Roscuro tried again. In honor of the occasion, the rat had borrowed a spoon from the tray and wore it on his head like a knight's helmet. He bowed with a long, sweeping gesture.

"Is that you, my little mouse?" Pea asked, moving toward the voice.

Roscuro winced. "I'm not a mouse," he said. "I'm a — a —"

"Oh, I forgot," said Pea, smiling. "You are my little gentleman, aren't you? Have you come to tell me how the story ends? Did you finish your quest? Where are you?"

From behind the perfume bottle, Roscuro stood taller. "I've come to apologize."

"You are noble, remember? You have nothing to be sorry about," she said, still searching.

"But I am," said Roscuro. "I am sorry." The rat stepped out from behind the perfume bottle and bowed low to Princess Pea. Slowly, gallantly, he raised his head to her.

"AHHHH! A RAT!" she screamed.

"No, no," said Roscuro, alarmed.

"NO . . . AH . . . NO!"

"Please, please, please listen," Roscuro said.

"AHHHHH! A RAT! Someone, please! AHHHH!" Pea hollered. "THERE IS A RAT

IN MY ROOM! HELP! HELP ME!
PLEASE—!"

"Listen, listen. Please listen. . . . It's OK. It's
all right. . . . Please listen."

Pea took a deep breath. And then—
"AHHHHHHHHHHH!"—she screamed
again and stumbled backward across the
room. The princess seized a poker and swung
wildly at Roscuro.

At the rat's size, the poker was terrifying.
He scrambled out of the way as the gigantic
iron rod whipped past his head, knocking
perfume bottles off the dresser. The spoon fell
off of Roscuro's head as he fled from the
Princess's room.

"IT'S A RAAAAAAAAAAAT!" she
screamed.

Roscuro ran as fast as he could down the
hallway. But the palace guards had heard Pea's
screams and they were running faster. Their
metal boots clanged on the stone floor as they
chased after him.

Roscuro darted out an open window and clung desperately to the ivy growing on the castle's walls. It was here that the rat made a terrible mistake. He looked down. It was a five-hundred-foot drop to the moat below. The sight of it made Roscuro's head spin.

Above him, the guards were already approaching the window.

Roscuro sped down the wall, swinging from vine to vine. But he couldn't help it. He looked at the moat once more and felt woozy all over again.

He closed his eyes for a moment, and then Roscuro's worst fear was realized. He lost his grip. The rat was falling, rushing toward the moat at a dizzying speed.

He reached for the wall, for anything to stop his fall. At the last second, Roscuro grabbed a piece of ivy just before he hit a windowsill. The sill broke his fall hundreds of feet up in the air.

Roscuro panted in front of a filthy pane of

leaded glass. He tried to look inside, but it was opaque with years of grime. The rat climbed through the open window and hoped for the best.

He landed in a cluttered broom closet of the servants' wing. Roscuro crawled over mops, rags, and feather dusters. He finally found refuge beside a metal bucket and leaned against the side.

Roscuro closed his eyes, exhaled, and opened them again. A monstrous face glared at him. The startled rat flinched — and then he realized he was looking at his own reflection.

Rat! the queen had shrieked. *Rat!* the princess had screamed.

What would you do if your own name was a bad word? If John, or Beth, or Bill was an insult? Well, that's how Roscuro came to feel about who he was.

But this time, the rat did not cry. This time, the rat stared at his reflection as if looking into a mirror. The face was mottled and distorted.

And when Roscuro emerged from the closet, all that could be seen of him were two beady, red eyes in the dark.

When your heart breaks, it can grow back crooked. It can grow back twisted, gnarled, and hard. The rat still had longing, but now he just longed for someone whose heart was as hardened as his was.

He scurried into the cluttered and windowless servants' wing. He glanced from side to side and darted along a wall, stealthily— like the rat he truly was.

The rat was searching, searching for someone. . . .

CHAPTER TWENTY-SIX

A Plan

Miggery Sow sat at the homemade dressing table in her room.

"Pretty princess," said Mig. "Pretty, pretty princess pie."

Only there wasn't a princess in sight, and Pea's belongings were long gone.

Mig looked straight ahead into a large wooden frame propped upon her table. She appeared to be gazing into a mirror. But it wasn't a mirror at all.

"What a *pretty princess*," said Mig, staring at the portrait of Princess Pea that had hung in the hallway. "*My* gloves. *My* comb. *My* pretty, spritzy water, all fresh and ladylike."

From a pipe in the corner, the rat watched the servant girl talk to herself. He watched her gaze at the stolen portrait of the princess as if it were her own reflection. He watched the girl *believe*. From the shadows, the rat saw all of this.

"My jewelly, girly hat, all sittin' on my princess head," Mig said. And with that, Miggery Sow took a spoon and sliced the painting right down the center of the canvas. "Who's the pretty, princess pumpkin pie?"

"You are," said a voice.

The rat settled upon her shoulder.

"Right," said Mig, not noticing the rat at all. "I *am*."

Roscuro whispered into Mig's ear. "You are. And you should be dressed in those clothes."

"Quite right, I should," she said.

"And you should lounge in that bed," Roscuro suggested.

"Loungin'," Mig repeated, delighted by the word. "Loungin' 'round . . . yes . . . the whole day."

"And *you* should be wearing that crown."

Mig cocked her head. "I should be wearin' a frown?"

"No," Roscuro said, sighing. "Not a frown. A *crown*."

"Gor!" Mig cursed. "Can't hear me ownself *think*!"

Then she did think. For a moment, at least. And she realized she hadn't been listening to her own inner voice at all, but to whatever was sitting upon her shoulder.

"AHHHHHHH!" screamed Miggery Sow.

"SHHHHHHH!" said Roscuro.

"AHHHHHHH!" she screamed again.

Roscuro put both paws to the girl's lips. "SHHHHHHH!"

"Who are you?" asked Mig.

"I'm here to help you," said Roscuro.

"By gettin' me caught with a real rat in me bunk. I don't think so," she said, and inhaled to scream again.

Roscuro threw his whole rat body against her mouth. "And what if they find you with a painting of the princess?" asked Roscuro slyly. "You think that's as bad as a rat?"

Mig paused. She thought, as best she could, while Roscuro eased backward.

"I want the same thing that you do," he said.

That night, Chef André sat alone in the spotless royal kitchen and played solitaire at his large table. Since the end of the days of soup, he had become a master at the game.

André was about to turn a card when he heard something. A thump from a distant corner. Followed by a soft "Oof!" Someone was in his kitchen.

"Allo?" he asked.

The noise stopped. He picked up his candle and walked toward the sound. The outline of a lumpy person holding a familiar object emerged from the shadows.

"Ahhh!" screamed André.

"Ahhh?" the girl asked.

"Ahhh!" he screamed again.

"Ahhh!" she screamed.

Holding his candlestick aloft with a shaking hand, André approached the trespasser. The light of his candle revealed a girl gripping a butcher knife. She turned to him and smiled.

"What are you doing?" André asked.

"Uh . . ." Mig said. "I need it for a baby."

André looked horrified.

Roscuro, tucked within the collar of Mig's shirt, leaned forward. "No!" he hissed into the girl's useless ears. "Not a baby! For *milady*!"

"I mean," Mig said loudly, "for milady."

The chef nodded.

Mig paused before saying more. "To chop apples. She'd like some apples."

André shrugged.

Mig stared, frozen.

"Now turn and leave," Roscuro instructed.

"Now turn and leave," Mig told André.

"No, no," Roscuro said, with a groan. "Just turn and leave."

"Oh, right. Sorry," Mig said to her collar. "Sorry . . . bye . . . I can't hear you . . . because . . . see . . ."

Miggery Sow's cheeks reddened as she turned to leave. But not before she wrapped the butcher knife in a kitchen towel and thrust it into her bag.

CHAPTER TWENTY-SEVEN

Gregory's Princess

You know, hurt is a funny thing. The same thing that makes one person angry can make another person grieve.

Not so many years ago, a man held his own bundle wrapped in a towel. But the towel wasn't wrapped around a butcher knife. It swaddled a baby.

"Take care of me little princess," the man said faintly. "I can't no more." Sobbing, the man handed the baby over to a rough-looking pig farmer named Ned.

"Oh, I will. Don't worry," Ned promised as the man reached down to kiss and stroke the head of his little girl for the last time. The man took the baby in his arms again and gave her one more tremendous hug.

"I'm sorry, sorry, so, so sorry," he said, weeping.

To be truthful, the baby was not a sweet-looking baby. Nor darling or dear or any of those other adjectives people use when cooing in unnaturally high-pitched voices. No, this baby was, to put it mildly, homely. It had a puffy, round face and a nose that could more accurately be called a snout.

The man clutched his baby tightly, not wanting to let her go. When he finally handed her back to Ned, the towel fell away to reveal a heart-shaped birthmark on the baby's shoulder.

Gregory always said that she had too much heart. And that's why they had to put some of it on the outside.

But let's face it. It's hard to see something on your back. In fact, you can have a good heart and not even know it.

Years passed and the baby grew up.

In a darkened hallway of the castle, the girl pulled up her shawl and covered her heart-shaped birthmark. Sitting atop that same shoulder, a rat whispered into the girl's ear.

"You can do this. You know you can," said Roscuro.

"I know I can," she said.

"She belongs in the dungeon. And you belong in the palace. Like a princess," he reminded her.

"Like a princess," Miggery Sow repeated.

Pea was sitting at her window, wishing for rain to pour down from the dark, dismal sky, when from somewhere behind her came a soft rustling. Pea hardly cared who it was or what they wanted, but she turned anyway.

The princess wasn't expecting the servant girl. And she certainly wasn't expecting Mig to be carrying a bundle of rope and so many odd-looking tools.

"What are you doing?" Pea asked.

Mig hesitated. "Cleaning, ma'am."

Roscuro rolled his eyes.

"With rope?" Pea asked.

"Helps, ma'am."

"Well, stop it," Pea said. "You look ridiculous."

"Sorry, ma'am?" said Mig, unable to hear Pea's soft voice.

"I said," Pea said louder, *"you look ridiculous!"*

Mig's ruddy cheeks whitened. Pea's words had reached Mig's damaged ears loud and clear. In fact, they seemed to arrive in slow motion, each syllable perfectly enunciated. Three stabs to Miggery Sow's heart: *YOU. LOOK. RIDICULOUS.*

Mig dropped the tools. She stared at the princess. Her face began to change colors. First pink, then grapefruit, and finally a deep crimson. Mig began to shake.

Squeezing the rope tight in her hand, Mig closed in on the princess.

Miggery Sow used every inch of rope. She wrapped and wrapped and wrapped until Princess Pea was one large coil.

And while the rest of the castle slept, the servant girl pressed a butcher knife to the princess's back and forced her down the stairs and into the foul, black dungeon.

"You can't do this, Mig," said Pea, trembling.

"Gor!" said Mig. "Seems I am, ma'am."

"You'll get in a terrible amount of trouble," Pea said.

"Don't listen," Roscuro whispered from inside Mig's collar. "*You're* the princess now."

"I'm the princess now," Mig repeated.

"And you belong in the palace," Roscuro said.

"And I belong in the palace," Mig said.

"And *she* belongs in . . ." Roscuro said, looking around in the darkness. *Yes, she belongs right here*, he thought.

Mig dragged Pea to a cell deep within the dungeon.

Behind the cell's bolted door, a lamp shone on the two figures — the golden-haired Pea, wrapped from head to toe in rope, and the dull servant girl, holding a butcher knife.

One was a princess. And one was not.

Pea looked around at her new home. "NO!" she screamed. "YOU CAN'T DO THIS! HELP! HELP! SOMEONE, HELP ME!"

"Tell her it's no use," Roscuro said to Mig. "No one can hear her."

"HELP! HEELLLLLLLP!" cried Pea.

"It's no use, ma'am," repeated Mig. "No one can hear you."

Ah, but someone could.

CHAPTER TWENTY-EIGHT

The Mouse's Quest

From a nook in the dungeon wall, two extraordinarily large ears turned — first right, then left — toward a distant sound.

Despereaux wrapped himself in a cloak and fled from his hiding place toward the cry for help. Hidden under his hood, he blended into the horde, one mouse in a sea of rats. Only his ears threatened to give him away. They bulged under his hood, but Despereaux quickly pulled them down.

Somehow, above the din of rats shouting and paws squelching on the slimy dungeon stone, Despereaux heard the cry again.

"Help! Help!"

Then he heard a second voice. "Hellllllp! I'm in here!"

The mouse looked up. The cries were coming from the prison cells. Despereaux ran closer, passing one cell door after another. He turned a corner and saw even more doors. But which one?

"Help!" someone cried from down the dark corridor. Miggery Sow's face was pressed against a barred window. "You filthy stinking rat! You tricked me!"

A large cluster of rats gathered in front of the cell next to Mig's, but they weren't paying the slightest attention to her. They were laughing at the sound of another prisoner weeping. To a rat, there is nothing more amusing than the suffering of others.

"It's a human, it's a human," said one, rubbing his paws together.

"Not yet, lads," ordered the largest among them. "Now, now. You've got to wait. It's nowhere near dinnertime."

"Oooh. Come on, Smudge," a rat replied. "I'm starving."

Another whimper came from the cell next to Mig's. Despereaux recognized it at once, and his tiny heart skipped a beat.

Pea.

The mouse studied the princess's locked door. It had a tiny slit of a window high above his head, far too high to reach. Despereaux scanned the corridor. Behind the rats, a broomstick was propped against a wall.

Perhaps Despereaux *had* learned a thing or two in school about being a mouse, because where a human would see a tool used for sweeping floors, the mouse saw a different use. He saw transportation. He raced to the top of the broom handle and pushed himself away from the wall, propelling it to the other side. The broomstick swung high over the heads of the oblivious rats.

"Something special for dinner tonight," a rat said from down below.

"It's a princess!" said another, pushing forward.

"Oy, oy," said Smudge. "You'll wait for dinner like everyone else."

Despereaux landed silently on the ledge next to Pea's door and leaped to her window.

"Milady!" Despereaux whispered.

Pea cried softly.

"Psst . . . MILADY!"

Startled, the princess turned and looked out the window. Her eyes darted toward Despereaux. "Oh, my little mouse! It's you!"

"I will deliver you from this evil, ma'am," Despereaux whispered. He was inches away from her.

"Oh, no," Pea whispered back. She tried to move, but she could not. She was still one big coil of rope. So instead the mouse pressed closer to her. He took in the sweet scent of her hair, her breath. . . . He would do anything for her.

"Just go find my father," Pea said. "Take this chain from around my neck to show him you are honest and truthful."

"Oh, I *am*," said Despereaux. "Honest and truthful and loyal and—"

"I know," Pea said. "But hurry! Here. Take it. There isn't much time."

Despereaux unhooked the chain, adorned with a heart-shaped gold locket, and took it from around her neck. The necklace was delicate on Pea, but it weighed heavily on the mouse. He held the heart in front of his own and draped the chain around him like armor.

"It will be my quest," he said.

"Thank you, my good gentleman," said Pea.

It was all Despereaux needed. Because a mouse needs *something* to push him through a mob of rats, through a dark and stinky dungeon, and toward inevitable doom.

He was a noble knight off to save his princess, and time was running out.

CHAPTER TWENTY-NINE

Heart

Despereaux hurried back to his nook and pulled back the brick. He ran through the chink in the wall and into the shaft of light. But in the mouse's haste, he fell — *poof!* — flat on his nose into a pile of soot. And when he got to his feet again, he was covered from head to tail in white dust.

The dust-covered mouse did not notice his ghostly appearance. Instead he focused on the pallid trace of light, his only link with the world above. He knew what he had to do — follow the light up and out of the chimney

shaft, no matter how far. And looking skyward, he knew that the climb would be nearly
impossible.

Despereaux began to scale the bricks. Up,
up, up, he climbed toward the light, not
stopping for a moment.

But the shaft's bricks angled back over
him, and after a while, he couldn't go any farther. He was close to the top, but there was
nothing more to grab onto.

Despereaux stopped on a small ledge and
looked down at the princess's locket in his
paws. He did not know how to go on. He
knew only that he *must* go on.

And then the mouse had an idea.

He took the princess' chain from around
his waist and swung it like a grappling hook.
He flung it as high as he could until the heart
caught on a crack in the mortar. Despereaux
yanked hard, and the heart caught fast.

The mouse grabbed the chain, took a deep
breath, and leaped off of the ledge. He swung

into the air, dangling in the darkness. Slowly, he began to pull his little body skyward. Paw over paw, inch by inch, he fought his way to the light.

Despereaux clutched the shaft's top brick with his little paw, and with great effort, he pulled himself out and into a crawlspace. And when the mouse stood and wrapped the chain around his waist again, he realized he had accomplished something unbelievable.

He had escaped from the dungeon.

But as soon as Despereaux raised his head, he saw that a more perilous challenge still lay ahead of him.

Now really, did you expect things to be that easy?

The mouse stood on the edge of the gaping hole he'd just crawled out of. The only way to make it over the shaft was to cross a long, narrow plank that stretched over it like a bridge. And every inch of this bridge was covered in mousetraps.

Despereaux swallowed hard. The traps went on as far as he could see. So many of them. A jumble of springs and bars waiting to break his neck. And falling off the bridge would be just as fatal.

Despereaux placed a paw on the gold heart around his waist and closed his eyes. Then he opened them again. He had come this far. He backed up a couple of steps, and then with a burst, the mouse ran forward.

Yes, the little mouse *ran*.

He hurtled himself at the traps, setting them off one after another.

SNAP! SNAP! SNAP!

Despereaux twisted, turned, and somersaulted, tripping one trap with an ear, triggering another with his tail. He used every bit of skill and experience to dance through the line of traps. All at once, there was a flurry of flying springs and more snapping metal. Bits of cheese flew into the air and dropped down the shaft.

SNAP! SNAP! SNAP! SNAP!

The last trap just missed the mouse's tail, and Despereaux's stomach dropped as the bar closed upon the necklace instead. With a final snap, the trap flew into the air, taking the necklace with it.

Despereaux lunged for the golden heart, but it slid though his fingers. He watched as Pea's heart disappeared into the blackness.

In the mouse's absence, every seat of the coliseum had been filled.

A few plump-bellied rats lounged in the royal box. It was a luxurious setting. An enormous magnifying glass rose decoratively from the box's roof, and, inside, servants fanned Botticelli and his guests with feathers and offered platters of food. Roscuro reclined among them like a king.

"Here you are, sir. Fresh worms," said a servant, holding out a bowl to Roscuro.

"Oh, um . . . " Roscuro said, lost in his own thoughts. "Thank you."

He tried to enjoy the worm, but his heart wasn't in it. He was listening to the cheers below.

"Well done, Roscuro," said Botticelli. "You hear that? That's all because of you. Come, my friend. Look at your handiwork."

Roscuro looked out at the spectacle. Hundreds of tiny orange lights glowed in the stands, and torchlight washed over the coliseum floor. The audience looked with anticipation at an arched doorway, where on either side, a line of rats drummed a slow and steady beat.

Pa-ruum, pa-ruum, pa-ruum.

Do you remember this sound? If you do, then you already know that what follows can't be good.

And it was not.

What emerged from the doorway was a shocking sight. A team of rats rolled out a large figure tied to a board with an intricate lattice of rope. It was a human, and her entrance made the coliseum explode in applause.

The rats cheered as Princess Pea was pulled to the center of the coliseum floor.

CHAPTER THIRTY

Not Dead

The king sat in his chambers, playing the sad and beautiful song for his dead queen. At the same time, high on a ledge above the king's shoulder, a mouse tried desperately to get his attention.

"King, King . . . Sire!" Despereaux cried, waving his arms. "Your daughter is in danger! Your Highness, please, sir!"

The king did not hear a word.

"Oh, come on," Despereaux said with a groan. He grabbed his ears and jumped off the ledge and into the air. Spreading his ears wide to slow his descent, the mouse glided down toward the king and circled him like a buzzing bee.

"Hey, Sire! Your Highness! Hello, Mr. King!" Despereaux yelled as he flew past the king's nose. "Hey! Hello. . . . Whoa." He circled around again and landed on the king's shoe. And still, the king took no notice.

Despereaux screamed as loud as he could from the foot of the king's chair. He jumped up and down. He tugged on the king's robes. All to no avail.

"Down here!" Despereaux shouted. "Down here! Listen, your daughter is in danger. She is locked in the dungeon. You are the only one who can help. She sent me to get you. Sir, please, sir!"

But the king just continued strumming his guitar.

"Sire! Your Highness! Look down here!" Despereaux pleaded.

What the mouse could not see was that

the king had begun to cry. A tear rolled to the edge of his cheek and fell to the ground.

When you are a mouse, a human tear can be pretty big. Imagine, if you will, a bathtub filled with water. And now imagine that tub being emptied from the top of a very tall building and onto your feet. Well, that is what the king's tear was like to Despereaux. "Oh!" said the mouse. He leaped out of the way when the tear landed next to him with a walloping *splat.*

And the thing about tears is, one is usually followed by another.

In the mouse world, an older mouse, who knew a lot about tears, walked through the center of town. His shoulders slumped and his head hung down. He looked a hundred years old, although he was much younger.

He was Lester Tilling. The only thing that ages a mouse more than time is grief.

Looking more weary than ever, Lester unlocked his front door. He shuffled inside listlessly and looked up. He froze. His mouth dropped open.

"Ah, ah . . . ahhhhh." Lester quivered.

"Dad! Dad," said Despereaux. "Listen. You've got to help me."

Despereaux stood in front of his father.

Lester trembled. "B-b-but y-y-you're dead."

You could not blame the mouse for thinking so. Still covered in white dust, Despereaux looked like a spirit risen from the depths of the dungeon.

"No, no, I'm not," said Despereaux. "I'm not dead. Now listen, the princess is in danger. She's locked in the dungeon."

Lester let out long choking sobs. "Oh my golly. You're de-de-dead." Then Lester Tilling keeled over and fainted.

"Dad," said Despereaux, shaking his father. "Dad, I'm not dead. Dad, Dad! Wake up! PLEASE!"

Despereaux ran out the front door for help, just as Furlough came sauntering up the walk.

"AHHHHHHHHHHHHHHHHHH!" Furlough screamed.

"Furlough, listen. You gotta help me!"

"You're de-de-de-de-"

"No, no, I'm not dead," Despereaux said. "Listen, the princess is in danger. She's locked in the dungeon."

Furlough raised his paws into the air. "Oh, my God. You're deaaaaaaaaaad!" He turned and scurried in the other direction.

"NO!" Despereaux yelled, watching his brother disappear. Wasn't there anyone who could help him?

On the other side of the street, three young mice he used to play with walked by.

"Guys, listen," Despereaux said soothingly. "OK, look. Now, I'm not dead—"

The mice gasped.

"The princess is in danger and she's down

in the dungeon—" But the mice were already backing away. They turned and fled. Despereaux chased after them. "You've got to help me!"

They were gone. The street was deserted. In fact, as Despereaux looked around, he noticed the entire town square was empty. In all of the mouse world, there was not a mouse to be seen.

"Somebody!" Despereaux shouted.

Looking about him in panic, he spotted his last chance to find help. He had to get to the bell tower. In a flash, Despereaux ran inside and up the stairs. At the top landing, the bell's long cord hung in the center. Despereaux jumped and grabbed for it. His weight pulled the rope down, and he dropped into a hole and straight to the base of the tower.

CLANG!

"Whoa!" Despereaux said.

The tips of his toes barely touched the ground before the rope sprung him back into the air again. He hung on tight as he shot to the tower's top floor. His head just missed the giant bell.

CLANG!

The bell echoed in this ears at a deafening pitch. Despereaux sank to the ground once more and bounced to the ceiling.

CLANG!

The bell resounded throughout the empty streets. But not one mouse answered its call. Instead they peeked out of their hiding spots to watch the small window at the top of the bell tower, where Despereaux Tilling popped up again . . . and again . . . and again.

CHAPTER THIRTY-ONE

The Chef Awakens

Elsewhere in Dor, another bell was ringing. It was calling people to a feast. Villagers flocked to the center of town, where a lavishly set table awaited them under a shining sun.

Baskets of fruit; wheels of cheese; sausages; roasted pheasants; sweet cakes of figs, dates, and prunes; and more delicacies piled high atop the table. The food seemed to go on forever, and the bell's toll invited all to enjoy it.

CLANG! CLANG! CLANG!

"Oh . . . um . . . oh!" André murmured. The chef sat aone in the royal kitchen. His eyes were closed and he slurped as if relishing the most scrumptious meal. "Ha, ha, ha!"

When André woke, the dinner bell was still ringing in his head. Was he imagining it? Or did he hear clanging on the other side of the wall? André glanced toward the mouse-hole just as the noise stopped.

The chef looked around his quiet kitchen. It was cold. And empty. The feast had been nothing but a dream.

"Enough," he said, jumping to his feet.

André pulled a knife from a large wooden block. He grabbed some carrots. He reached for some celery stalks, a few tomatoes, and, of course, garlic. He chopped with fast, expert movements. His hand was a blur. *Whack, whack, whack!*

"Ha, ha," André said, laughing to himself. "Yes."

The chef dumped the chopped ingredients into a gleaming stockpot. A rich broth began to simmer. André leaned forward and smelled the aroma, as comforting as a long-lost friend.

"Ah!" he sighed, inhaling the fragrant steam that danced above the pot.

The smell of soup traveled from the royal kitchen to the other rooms. It drifted into every corner of the castle. It rose into chimneys and pipes and wafted out into the streets.

In the lifeless square below, a sleepy villager was sitting on a stoop when the scent tickled his nostrils. His eyes widened. He stopped, then sniffed. By the man's feet, his dog sniffed, too. The man and the dog looked at each other. It had been a long time, but they knew that smell.

But there was something else. The villager felt a familiar sensation. Was it . . . could it be? He looked in disbelief at the sky. He felt it again. He stuck his hand out, and then he was sure. He actually felt it!

A raindrop.

André grabbed more cloves of garlic and merrily flung them into the pot.

Just over his shoulder, the pages of his cookbook stirred, as if a gentle breeze had passed through the room. Fruit and vegetables of every kind sprung from the book. They rose above the table and formed into Boldo's smiling face. The genie looked over André's shoulder and inspected the bubbling pot of soup.

"Look at you!" Boldo said. "You're still brewing tea."

André spun around.

"If you want to make a statement, what do I say?" Boldo said, pointing a string-bean finger at André. "Make it a good one!"

André smiled at his old friend.

"It's so great to see you," Boldo said.

"Fantastic!" André said, throwing himself into Boldo's arms. André and Boldo embraced and, without missing a beat, got to work.

"Marjoram?" André asked.

"Love it," Boldo said. "Perfect."

"Ah! *Bellissima.*"

Raindrops pattered against the kitchen windows. Small puddles formed in the streets. Dorians all over the kingdom opened their windows and doors to have a look.

People filled the square and pointed their faces toward the sky, feeling the cool drops for the first time in ages. And then their noses twitched. The villagers inhaled the soup's aroma.

In the mouse village, Despereaux's nose twitched, too. He sniffed again and wondered where the smell was coming from.

The royal kitchen was becoming the wonderful mess it once was. Shiny pots and pans were replaced by tomato splats, carrot tops, corn husks, and onion peels.

And in the cooking frenzy, Boldo grew

and grew and grew with excitement — to twice the size he was before.

"Cauliflower?" André asked.

"Perfect," Boldo replied.

"Some celery?"

"Good."

The pair was so enthralled by their latest creation that neither the chef nor the genie noticed the small visitor who had entered through the mousehole and was trying to catch their attention.

"Hey! Hello!" Despereaux called up to them.

"Celery. Parsnips," Boldo said.

"Down here!" Despereaux cried by André's feet.

André consulted Boldo before adding another ingredient.

"THE PRINCESS IS IN DANGER!" yelled Despereaux.

"Garlic, did I use garlic?" Boldo asked.

Despereaux was about to scream at the top of his little mouse lungs when his eye caught something twinkling on the kitchen floor. Amid the scraps of hacked-up produce lay a small needle.

André tasted the soup.

"Brav — OWWWWWWW!" he cried, wincing.

The chef grabbed his foot and peered down at the mouse who had just stabbed it.

"The princess is in danger!" Despereaux yelled, holding the needle like a sword.

André leaned in close, his face as large as a giant's. "Oh, you are a cute little mouse. Would you like some soup?" André's huge hand reached down and picked up the mouse by the tail.

Despereaux hung upside down. "No, I don't want—" he said indignantly. "The princess is in danger!"

"And a talking mouse, too," André said.

"Listen, you've got to help me!"

"Perhaps a little cheese?" André asked, setting Despereaux down upon the table.

"No, I don't want any cheese!" Despereaux hollered. "The princess is in danger! She's locked in the dungeon!"

Boldo gasped. "In the dungeon?"

"Oh, don't be silly, my little mouse," André said. "Everything is fine. The princess is perfectly safe up in her — "

BOOM!

A huge thunderclap shook the castle. Andre went to the window. He marveled at the miracle unfolding in front of them.

BOOM!

The thunder echoed throughout the land.

"Oh, my," André said, staring out the window. He turned back to the kitchen. "Boldo, look! It's — "

But the kitchen was empty. The only movement was a swirl of steam rising from the soup pot.

"Boldo?" André looked around. "Old friend? Where are you?"

CHAPTER THIRTY-TWO

The Battle Begins

Despereaux and Boldo hurried toward the dungeon's stairs.

"CHAAARRRRRGE!" the mouse cried from Boldo's shoulder.

With each step, the genie grew larger and larger, and the mouse rose higher and higher. Until, at seven feet tall and armored entirely in kitchenware, the genie looked like the proudest of knights. He wore a mixing bowl as a helmet and a roasting pan as a chest plate. In his hand, he brandished a long rotisserie skewer with a roasted chicken still speared to its end.

"Tell me again," Boldo said.

"Chivalry! Bravery! Honor!" Despereaux said, raising his needle into the air.

"CHIVALRY! BRAVERY! HONOR!" Boldo repeated. He thrust his skewer sword with a laugh. "Ha, ha! I just love to be out of the kitchen!"

The genie dashed down the corridor.

"Into the breach!" he cried.

Despereaux clung on tight as Boldo descended the many flights of stairs to the deepest part of the dungeon.

"Down this way," Despereaux said at the last step. He pointed in the direction of the cells.

"*Andiamo.* Charge!" Boldo shouted.

They turned down the dark corridor.

"There. That way." The mouse motioned toward where he'd last seen Pea. Her door was ajar.

"HA!" Boldo cried, leaping in front of the princess's cell. They peered inside.

"But she was . . ." Despereaux said.

They were too late. Pea's cell was empty.

In the packed coliseum, Botticelli's booming voice drew the rats' attention away from the princess pinned to the floor. They looked up at the royal box in anticipation.

"My friends! My friends!" Botticelli cried, placing a paw on Roscuro's shoulder. "There are rats, and then there are . . . *rats!*"

The rowdy audience raised their fists into the air and roared.

"And now," Botticelli continued, turning toward Roscuro. "I would like a huge round of applause for our good friend here, for delivering us our *princess!*"

The rats welcomed their new hero with a thundering ovation. There was no denying it.

Roscuro was now utterly and unmistakably a rat. His reception could be heard in every corner of the dungeon.

In the distance, Despereaux cupped an ear at the sound.

"Come on, let's go!" he ordered Boldo. They bolted past the cells, following the applause.

"Oy, hang on," Mig called through the bars of her window. "Where are you going? Help!"

But Boldo and Despereaux were already marching toward the bridge that lead to the coliseum.

"Hurry!" Despereaux cried.

They did not see the many glowing red dots blinking in the darkness. The rats were watching.

"Oh," said one, licking his chops at the sight. "Look at that."

"Let's get him!" said another.

At his cry, hundreds of rats poured forth from the shadows of the dungeon's hall. They looked like an army. As one, they ran at the genie.

"Ah!" Boldo cried as the army attacked.

He tried to move forward, but the rats crawled all over him. They climbed up his legs and into his armor, gnawing away at every limb and joint.

"Keep going," Despereaux urged.

A rat raced up Boldo's shoulder and lunged for the mouse. But Despereaux was ready. He wielded his needle like a battle-ax, whacking away as bravely as any full-sized knight. The rat tumbled to the floor.

A second rat followed, and then another. From every side, rats pounced with open jaws. Despereaux kicked a fat one, pushing him to the ground. He tossed another. He jabbed and blocked, just as he'd done in the library. Only these were not imaginary enemies. The rats were frighteningly real, and one by one, the mouse's blows threw them to the dungeon floor.

But it was too late for Boldo.

The rats bit into his foot with a loud *crunch,* and the genie crashed down the stairs. When Despereaux saw him again, the valiant knight was just a long trail of pots and pans.

CHAPTER THIRTY-THREE

A Chain of Remarkable Events

A ball of light bounced down the dungeon corridor. Gregory the jailer was holding his lamp while making his rounds. His feet rhythmically clomped on the stone, and his ring of keys jangled with each step. He stopped and looked around.

"Mmm nnn hrrrr!" a muffled voice called.

Gregory tilted his head. Did he hear something?

"I'mmmm inn herrrre!"

Gregory's ears perked up. He walked back to a cell door and peeked through its small window. He saw a girl crouched in the corner of the dingy cell. Or what he thought was a girl, anyway. With her back to the jailer, she looked more like a mountain of rags.

"HELLLLLLLLLLLLLLLP! I'm in here!" she screamed into a grate in the floor.

Gregory placed a key into the lock and pushed the door open. He stepped inside to get closer. The girl wept, not seeing him enter. The jailer raised his lantern, and the beam of light fell upon the top of her left shoulder. Gregory struggled to hold the lantern steady. His hands shook as the light hovered—directly upon the girl's heart-shaped birthmark.

The jailer dropped his ring of keys.

"Gor," Mig said, turning around at the sound. "What took you so long? I've been screamin' in here for hours!"

It's strange to think that the Dorians who gathered outside the castle walls had no idea about the chain of remarkable events occurring within. Not the father-daughter reunion in the dungeon, nor the mouse's quest, not even the capture of their princess, who was about to become dinner.

You see, at that moment, the people of Dor were experiencing their own rather remarkable series of events.

The villagers had felt the rain and they had smelled the soup. And now, behind them, a single ray of light was breaking through the clouds.

"Look, Pa! There!" said a boy, pointing to the sky. "Up there!"

The others turned toward the light. And then, all together, the villagers raised their faces toward the sun.

But the king, at his window, looked down. He gazed out at the smiling faces cleansed by the rain and warmed by the sun, and he smelled the aroma of soup brewing. And a tear formed in the corner of his eye. The king had forgotten. He had forgotten the smiles and the soup, the rain and the sun — and all of it sparked a flicker of life in his sad heart.

Despereaux opened his eyes. He slowly got to his feet and looked around. The rats were gone. Boldo lay in pieces all over the floor.

The mouse was alone now. He hung his head in despair.

Nearby, something rustled. Despereaux looked up to see Boldo's hand stirring. It lifted slightly and pointed in the direction of the coliseum. Despereaux looked to Boldo's face, and as if reading the mouse's mind, the genie smiled.

The mouse was reminded that a knight must forge on — with bravery, chivalry, and honor.

And that is exactly what he did.

The coliseum crawled with rats eager to eat. Everywhere were pointed claws and scaly tails and long, dripping teeth. The rats leaned hungrily toward Pea, and the guards struggled to hold them back with long sticks.

"Wait. Wait just a moment," Botticelli told the crowd. "Patience. Not. Just. Yet."

He motioned to two of his rats who rolled out a giant gong for all to see. The crowd went wild, knowing the feast was about to begin.

"Ah, the honor is all yours, my friend," Botticelli said to Roscuro. He handed him a bone.

"EAT! EAT! EAT!" the rats chanted.

Roscuro took the bone in his paws and the chant grew louder.

"EAT! EAT! EAT!"

The rat raised the bone into the air.

CHAPTER THIRTY-FOUR

Time for Dinner

OK. Remember when we said that grief was the strongest thing a person could feel?

Well, it isn't.

It's forgiveness. Because a single act of forgiveness can change everything.

With the bone still tight in his paw, the rat looked deeply into the princess's eyes. And for the first time, the princess looked into the rat's. Sometimes you can tell someone you're sorry without saying a word.

Roscuro threw the bone to the ground.

"No," he said.

"What?" cried Botticelli. "Why, you worthless little —"

The chant grew louder. "EAT! EAT! EAT! EAT! EAT!"

Furious, Botticelli snatched up the bone and banged the gong himself. The crowd stormed the coliseum floor, trampling one another to be the first to get to Pea. Despereaux arrived just as the wave of rats rushed toward the princess.

"A H H H H H H H H H H H H H !" Pea screamed.

Despereaux gasped. What could a single mouse do against *this*? he thought, looking around the arena. Rats were everywhere. Some were already climbing onto the princess. The only thing free of rats was the cat's cage, tucked in a corner.

Despereaux looked at the top of the cage, where the large wheel that released the cat was left unguarded.

He wove through the mass of rats toward the cage. The cat, as if remembering the little mouse, hissed at Despereaux through the bars. It looked ravenous. And this time, the mouse welcomed the cat's hunger.

He climbed up the side of the cage and grabbed the wheel.

"AHHHHH!" Pea screamed again. Rats had already reached her neck and bared their fangs. They swarmed all over her.

Despereaux turned the wheel. The cage's door creaked open, and the cat squeezed through. It burst into the coliseum with a snarl as loud as a tiger's.

"*Whoooo* let him out?" Botticelli demanded.

The cat extended his claws and slashed at everything in his path. Each swipe sent rats flying into the air.

From the top of the cage, Despereaux watched the rats scatter and scream.

"Hey, you!" said a voice behind him.

Despereaux spun around. Towering over

him, two rats held bones over their heads like clubs. He grabbed his sword just as the rats swung. Despereaux blocked them both in one move.

"GET HIM!" Botticelli yelled, pointing Despereaux out to the others.

More rats armed with bones and spears raced to the top of the cage to join the fight. The mouse was surrounded.

"Ha!" a rat exclaimed, aiming his weapon at the mouse's feet. Despereaux hopped over it and retaliated with a jab that knocked the rat's hat off. Despereaux's sword was a blur, swiping in all directions.

Another rat struck at Despereaux and missed. But the others were closing in. They stabbed at the mouse with long spears and forks. Despereaux ducked and darted. He ran through the rats' legs and leaped on the wheel as more rats scrambled up the side of the cage.

The fight raged on, with the mouse and

several rats trying to balance on the wheel spinning underfoot.

Roscuro and Pea watched helplessly.

From the corner of his eye, Despereaux saw the wheel's handle and stepped on it. The wheel whizzed around at a blinding speed and sent the rats flying.

Despereaux was thrown, too. He dropped over the side of the cage. At the last moment, he caught the edge of the roof with his paw and hung on for his life.

Pea looked at Despereaux's feet swinging in midair. Her eyes widened in fear.

Using all his strength, the mouse raised his upper body over the side of the cage — to find someone waiting there for him.

"If it isn't our brave little knight," Botticelli said, sneering in the mouse's face. With one paw, he grabbed Despereaux by the neck and raised him above his head. "And it seems he came just in time for dinner."

"NO!" cried Pea.

"Hmm. I wonder . . ." said the rat, pulling a blade from his belt. "Should I finish you off myself or turn you into cat food?"

Botticelli dangled the mouse over the edge of the cage, where just below, the snarling cat snapped at the heels of the tasty offering.

CHAPTER THIRTY-FIVE

Light

It all began with one ray of light.

But sometimes one is enough. As the villagers watched, that one ray made room for more to slip between the gray clouds. Then the light forced the clouds apart and away entirely.

The sun took over the sky. It spread through the square, destroying the shadows and painting everything it touched with a rainbow of color.

Sunlight filled every crevice, including the chimney shaft. No longer a weak trickle, the light burst down the shaft to where Pea's fallen necklace still lay. The beam reflected off the gold locket and shot straight to the center of the rat world.

The cat jumped for the mouse, just missing him. One more try, and the little rodent would be his.

"Here, kitty, kitty, kitty!" Botticelli said, hanging Despereaux over the cat. "Here, kitty, kitty, kitt—AH!"

Botticelli winced as if in pain.

"What is THAT?" Botticelli asked. He squinted at the light seeping through the hole in the wall.

Light illuminated the rat village—the bones, the mounds of rotting trash, and the coliseum floor. The rats shielded their eyes and cowered.

Except for one.

In the light, Roscuro spotted the magnifying glass above the royal box. The rat knew what he had to do. He climbed to the top of the box. He pointed the glass toward the ray of sun and aimed a powerful blast of light toward the cage.

Botticelli was blinded. He released Despereaux and covered his eyes. He staggered backward, stepping right off the edge of the cage.

"AHHHHHH!" Botticelli screamed.

There was silence.

Despereaux peered down below. Botticelli lay on the coliseum floor.

But that wasn't the worst of it. As the rat lay on the floor, an enormous shadow crept over him.

The rat opened his eyes. "Ahhhhh! Please. Nice kitty. No! No! Noooooooooo!"

The tomcat raised a clawed paw.

Botticelli ran for the nearest shelter — the cat cage. The cat followed him in.

With one kick, Pea slammed the cage door shut. The force made the door's latch fall, and it locked. And then it was difficult to tell which was louder, the cat's snarls or the rat's long, tortured howl.

From the top of the cage, Despereaux looked down at his princess and smiled, and the princess smiled back. It was over, they thought.

But Roscuro was not finished. He swiveled the magnifying glass around, sending beams of light all over the dungeon. Screaming rats scurried into any darkness they could find, disappearing into cracks and holes, until the underground village was quiet and flooded with light.

Despereaux untied Pea. She sat up and smiled.

"Thank you, my good gentleman," she said.

Behind the mouse, someone sniffed. Despereaux and Pea turned to see the rat who had stayed behind.

Roscuro walked hesitantly up to Pea, and their eyes met again.

"I am sorry," said Roscuro.

"You have nothing to be sorry about," said the princess.

And with her words, the rat's heart softened. Just like that.

In another part of the dungeon, a father held the daughter he thought he'd lost forever.

"I am so, so sorry," Gregory said to Mig, hugging her tight. "You have no idea how sorry I am."

And Miggery Sow enjoyed the strange new feeling that lightened her heart.

And in his chambers, the king stood at his window, looking down at his subjects drenched in sunlight.

"I'm so sorry," said the king quietly, almost to himself.

His people cheered at the sight of him, and his kingdom once again glistened like a tiny jewel against the sea.

The king turned, as always, toward the painting of his queen.

And he smiled.

Epilogue

So you could call all of this a big misunderstanding if you wanted to.

A king was hurt, so he hurt a rat. And a rat was hurt, so he hurt a princess. And a princess was hurt, so she hurt a servant girl without even meaning to. And that servant girl had been hurting for so long that almost nothing could make her feel better.

But was it a mistake? Or was it just good luck?

Because the servant girl went back to her farm. And the jailer finally found his princess. And the king found something stronger than grief. And the mice finally got rid of their fear.

Miggery Sow got her very own tiara from Princess Pea herself. And Mig happily returned to her pigs as her father lovingly watched over her. And the king played a new tune just for his daughter. And young mice everywhere took up the new sport of running through obstacle courses of mousetraps while their parents *clapped*.

And the people of Dor lived side by side with their rats.

All except the one, who went back to sea and felt cool breezes each morning and sun on his face every afternoon.

And our small hero? Well, he had many more adventures to come. Because a valiant knight will always find adventure, even if he makes his own. And those who listened carefully could often hear the mouse's small cry of victory.

And we'd tell you that they all lived happily ever after. . . .

But what fun is that?

THE END

First edition 2008

Library of Congress Cataloging-in-Publication Data is available.

Library of Congress Catalog Card Number 2008932952

ISBN 978-0-7636-4076-7

2 4 6 8 10 9 7 5 3 1

Printed in the United States of America

This book was typeset in Garamond Ludlow Light.
The illustrations were created digitally.

Candlewick Press
99 Dover Street
Somerville, Massachusetts 02144

visit us at www.candlewick.com